Mark Leech was born in 1977 in Newcastle-under-Lyme, Staffordshire. He studied English at St Anne's College, Oxford and now lives in London where he works as an editor. He has a passionate interest in history and literature and was inspired to write *Unknown Soldiers* by the written accounts of French soldiers and their families. He has had a number of poems, short stories and articles published. This is his first novel.

UNKNOWN SOLDIERS

Mark Leech

Unknown Soldiers

Vanguard Press

VANGUARD PAPERBACK

© Copyright 2002
Mark Leech

The right of Mark Leech to be identified as author of
this work has been asserted by him in accordance with the
Copyright, Designs and Patents Act 1988

All Rights Reserved

No reproduction, copy or transmission of this publication
may be made without written permission.
No paragraph of this publication may be reproduced,
copied or transmitted save with the written permission or in
accordance with the provisions
of the Copyright Act 1956 (as amended).

Any person who does any unauthorised act in relation to
this publication may be liable to criminal
prosecution and civil claims for damage.

A CIP catalogue record for this title is
available from the British Library
ISBN 1 843860 09 0

*Vanguard Press is an imprint of
Pegasus Elliot MacKenzie Publishers Ltd.*
www.pegasuspublishers.com

First Published in 2002

**Vanguard Press
Sheraton House Castle Park
Cambridge England**

Printed & Bound in Great Britain

Dedication

For Claire

Ricard

Ricard was glad to leave Paris. As the long train pulled out of the station he leaned back from the window to conceal himself and his uniform from the people on the platform. There were too many eyes in Paris. He was always aware of them.

Sometimes they bored into him, several pairs at once. These were the eyes of demobbed soldiers. They stood in groups all round the wintry streets, some in stained fatigues, some in badly-darned civilian clothes, their hands in their pockets. Their faces were all the same – lined, sallow, tired. Ricard could not bring himself to look into their eyes for too long. They reminded him he was an alien. Now that they were no longer soldiers even the shared experience of uniform could build no rapport between him and them.

Sometimes the eyes were completely different. They flickered from him to other things, back to him as though drawn irresistibly, then away again. These were the eyes of women, old men, even of children. To them, Ricard supposed, soldiers *were* the war. The rationing and the dead, the disabled beggars who shuddered in filthy uniforms on wet pavements – all these things came from the soldiers. All soldiers, even ones sun-tanned and well-fed, bore part of the blame. He was not one of *those* soldiers, Ricard insisted to himself. It was plain enough that that he was not part of the war. But the neat blue of his captain's uniform was similar enough to the spoiled blue of the men who had returned from the Western Front. They would not accept Ricard enough even to look straight at him.

He began to relax as Paris slipped away from the windows. The compartment was empty but the door would not close properly and slammed continually as the train lurched into the countryside. There had been refugees on the platform, clutching possessions, children and, occasionally, animals. He had been able to separate himself from them by virtue of the fact that he was still in employment. They were all going to the same place as Ricard but, again, they would not look at him. He almost welcomed the slamming of the compartment door. It at least paid enough attention to him to annoy him.

Lulled by the gentle rocking of the train, he lit a cigarette, smoothed his dense moustache and sat upright in his seat to look out of the window. Paris was only a few minutes behind, but already signs of the war could be seen in the increasingly flat land. Here and there were pieces of military equipment slowly rusting: gun carriages, coils of barbed wire. Plants had begun to grow around and over them as though eager to press them back into the damp ground. Villages and towns appeared and disappeared, often bearing the scars of the Germans' near-victories of 1914 and 1918. Everywhere the people, the farmers attempting to clear their fields, townspeople, the refugees who could not afford to fit on to a train and now clogged the roads with their carts and horses, had bowed heads. All gazed relentlessly at the ground even when the smoke from the train engulfed them where they patiently waited at rail crossings. It was as through they carried the low grey clouds on their necks. Ungrateful, the clouds refused them even the cold relief of rain and remained, threatening.

Ricard saw all this with a kind of amazement. He had barely seen his own country since before the war. He had read about it, when newspapers had reached him, but it had seemed almost irrelevant. Now the journey eastward was giving him a rapid education. When he disembarked at Rheims in the cold of the following morning he almost believed that he himself was a victim of war.

The smell of it ran through Rheims. It was a damp, metallic smell that seemed to colour the walls of the tired-looking buildings Ricard could see during his few minutes outside. He could feel his own face growing pale as he hurried into the army depot on the outskirts of the town. The sergeant at the desk accepted his arrival without comment.

"Your name sir? Regiment? Sir?"

"Ricard Villier. Now attached to the Hundred and Fourth. I would like a horse, or some other transport. I have to take up a new post."

The sergeant ran a thin finger with a bruised nail down his list of instructions. He wiped his hand on his mouth and transferred the saliva to the front of his uniform.

"Yes. From the island of Grenon?"

"Yes."

"The CO would like to speak to you. Come this way sir."

Ricard was led through narrow corridors apparently made of decaying wood to a nondescript door with no markings on it. The sergeant paused and looked him up and down.

"Have you got a cigarette sir?"

"Er, yes, yes I have. Thank you, soldier."

The sergeant glanced up from the cigarette and his lips flickered momentarily into a sort of smile. Then he knocked at the door, turned on his heel and walked away down the corridor. The sound of his boots splashing through puddles on the hard floor disappeared. Ricard was left alone with the voice that emanated from behind the door.

"Come in."

As he sat astride his horse in the drizzle that even turned the wood, through which he and the column struggled, black, Ricard reflected on what he knew about the village of Pericard. He was grateful to the sergeant and Colonel Blamanchard for not looking at him as people had done in Paris. If he had not been, he would have tried to discipline the sergeant for his presumption in asking for a cigarette. The problem was, though they had not looked at him with the eyes of victims of war, they had looked at him with pity. Ricard was not used to pity. He had been captain of the garrison at Grenon! Such a thing, which would have brought him respect in 1914, was no longer important. Not in Pericard anyway, judging by what that the Colonel had told him. There had been something very odd in the Colonel's demeanour, he thought. He spoke quietly even though the strength of his voice had indicated that in normal circumstances he was a loud man.

"You are going to Pericard?"

"Yes sir."

"What orders do you have?"

"I don't really know. I was recalled for 'active service'. But the war is over."

"You will certainly be active."

The Colonel had looked up at him at this point, and smiled oddly behind his moustache. He reached into the pile of typewritten papers on a desk and pulled out a bulky package.

"These are your written orders. I don't think you'll have ever had anything like them before. I'd better add some verbal advice to them, I suppose."

He held out the package and paused. Ricard hesitated before taking it. Blamanchard's movements were all so – understated. Should he take it from him? Was he actually

14

handing it over? The package was not as heavy as it had looked. Ricard weighed it in his hand while he waited for the Colonel to start speaking again. The pause grew uncomfortably long and Ricard found himself staring over his superior's shoulder out of a dirty window into the courtyard of the barracks. He jumped, embarrassingly, when Blamanchard began to murmur again.

"Did you see any action in the Caribbean?"

"A little, sir."

"Pericard saw quite a lot. The front line barely moved until the spring of last year. And even then it took a lot of fighting to halt their advance. There's more of Pericard on the maps than there is on the ground. It is... a strange place."

Ricard nodded, not understanding. A place that only existed on maps would necessarily be strange. If it was even stranger than that... he restrained a shrug.

"Be careful. Do not disbelieve things that seem to be ridiculous. If you had served here... the Germans shelled Paris a year ago, but this time they didn't reach it. My point is that the war was strange, and there are strange places that it visited."

"Thank you sir."

"You will join the column of men returning from leave. And congratulations. Your orders include a promotion."

Ricard felt an excitement in him that jarred against the subdued mustiness of the Colonel's office. He brought himself to attention and saluted smartly.

"Thank you sir!"

The colonel smiled again, sadly this time, and twitched a finger in return. Then he stared for a long time at his subordinate. Ricard had felt uncomfortable under the watery grey eyes. There seemed to be a strange loneliness in them. He had been on the verge of clearing his throat to speak when Blamanchard had pre-empted him.

"You are a career soldier, I suppose."

"Yes, er… Yes I am."

"Are you happy with it? You hesitated."

"My – family didn't exactly approve. I haven't spoken to any of them for a long time."

"All alone in the world, eh? You remind me of one of my officers, Major Desailles. He is a career soldier too, though I think he has more experience than you do. Not in the last war, before that."

Blamanchard became quiet again. Ricard did not like the unnatural stillness of the man, though there was nothing unkind in his manner.

"If that's all, sir…"

He had left as hurriedly as was decent, for the first time regretting his habit of firm, correct salutes.

The excitement of becoming Major Villier had subsided on the long ride to Pericard. He had not yet had chance to look at his orders before setting off because the column of men was already waiting for him. He had exchanged a few words with the lieutenant in charge, a man who was at least ten years older than Ricard and had a dogged air. This had been embarrassing. The lieutenant's beard and hair were greying, and he had the creased skin of a man who felt every one of his forty-odd years. He made Ricard feel guilty about his own recent elevation far above what this man could expect.

Even so he appeared to go through life stolidly and Ricard did not expect to hear any complaints from him at any time.

He and his men had the same reserved air that had belonged to Blamanchard. They almost tiptoed along the soggy mud of the road, and Ricard began to feel that his movements were clumsy in comparison. It was as though despite the fact that the war had ended months ago they still had not yet got used to the quiet. They seemed to be afraid of noise in case any sound provoked the avalanche of guns again.

Ricard did not know much about the war, but his speculations were encouraged by what he could see. On either side of the road the scale of destruction terrified him. Things rusted or rotted together in heaps. Here and there tiny grey figures pulled on ropes or struggled with spades. Their efforts were dwarfed by the unending chaos that surrounded them. Ricard imagined small patches of tended ground appearing where they had worked, each little area needing to be fenced off from the sludge that threatened to overwhelm it. Even the long grass seemed to be stained with the ragged rust that clung to the used shell cases that lined either side of road in infinite numbers. A few birds chattered without enthusiasm wherever the stump of a tree emerged hesitantly into the air, but apart from this, all sound was replaced by smell.

Ricard could not place the smell. It reminded him of sweat, and it reminded him of the turtles that had died on the beaches of Grenon and lain in the sun for a few days. There was also metal in it. Not the silvery, efficient smell of clean rifle barrels, but something dustier, something that had collapsed from over-use.

The men that he rode alongside were no more pleasant to see than the surroundings. Ricard had liked to believe that he was not a harsh disciplinarian on Grenon, but any man among his twenty-five who had looked like these would have been clearing out the latrines and then removing the turtles from the beach. Their uniforms were creased and holed, stained with filth. Many of them trailed their rifles in the mud. All of them had the posture he had seen from the train on his way to Rheims. Shoulders bowed, eyes directed at the toes of their boots.

"Anyone would think we had lost the war."

He murmured this to himself. He did not want to attract any of those eyes to him. Not yet, anyway. From the terse words of the lieutenant he knew that they had all been conscripts, dragged into the war. He could understand, after having seen the eyes in Paris, why had they not yet dragged them themselves away from it, despite the very obvious misery of their existences.

The day had never emerged properly from the clouds and rain, and it was giving up the struggle with the dark when the lieutenant slowed his horse and dropped from the head of the column to come alongside Ricard. He pointed along the ground to where a group of indistinct structures huddled together in the gloom.

"Pericard, sir."

It was dark when they reached the village. Ricard presumed it wasn't the original village itself since what he could see of it centred around some wooden military buildings. Ricard was tired, too tired to peer into the murk to actually make out what he could half-see. He dismounted and gave the reins of his horse to a soldier who waited for him in the cold rain. Ricard could see an open door and light that was disconcertingly bright after the long day of gloom. The lieutenant stood beside this light, clasping his sodden greatcoat around his shoulders.

"This way, sir."

In the orange light of oil lamps he shuddered the cold out of his clothes and sat at a rough table. Food was brought to him and the lieutenant. Stew, warmed up, with lumps of meat. What kind of meat he had no idea, but it didn't seem to matter. Ricard pulled some bread from the coarse loaf next to his elbow and dipped it in the lukewarm stew. He wolfed down a couple of mouthfuls before remembering some form of civility.

"I am sorry, I haven't eaten all day. I'm afraid I don't know your name."

"Jannert, sir. Lieutenant Jean Jannert."

"You fought?"

"Yes sir. Not here though. At Verdun, and then the Somme. I was wounded there. I have only just returned from sick leave."

"Have you been to Pericard before? I was told that it was a strange place."

The lieutenant almost answered, but he was interrupted by the sentry snapping to attention at the open door to the hut. This movement was followed by the entry of two more officers, a captain and another lieutenant. They saluted Ricard and he invited them to sit down.

"Thank you, sir. I am Captain Henri Deschaves. This is my lieutenant Jacques Vellard. We have been in acting command here since the departure of our last major."

"What happened to him?"

"He went mad, sir."

Deschaves' face twitched as he spoke. The movement was accentuated by the shadows cast on his thin face by the lamps. Ricard almost believed that Deschaves was an old man, but beneath the lines of weariness, he was young and had an almost jovial air. Vellard was certainly younger. His cheeks still had the slight podginess of a plump child, and he had no moustache or even whiskers. His eyes wavered to and from a point on the side of Deschaves' head as though he was looking for guidance. He did not offer anything to the conversation.

"I was just enquiring from Lieutenant Jannert what he knew about Pericard."

Deschaves frowned.

"Have you no orders, sir?"

"I have only just returned from service overseas. I have not yet had chance to look at my orders. As you see, I still wear my captain's epaulettes."

He smiled at Deschaves to reassure him. He knew it

19

was a nervous smile – he could feel trembling in his lips as they stretched. Deschaves smiled back. Ricard breathed a sigh of relief. For the first time since he had arrived in France, someone had actually humanly communicated with him. The relaxation of tension in this moment created a wave of tiredness through him. He struggled manfully with it and listened again to what Deschaves was saying.

"I think, sir, that you should read your orders. Tomorrow I'll show you round. But for the moment, sir, would you like some wine with your meal?"

Ricard nodded, remembering his food. As Deschaves got to his feet to get a bottle he let his gaze wander over the interior of the hut. It was partly made of wood, partly of corrugated iron. The nails that held the structure in place still gleamed. Ricard supposed that it had only been built recently, after the end of the war.

"How far are we from the old front line?"

Jannert shook his head.

"I don't know."

Vellard looked at his superior officer with frightened eyes. His dirty fingers ran up and down the front of his uniform. Ricard frowned at him, trying to work out what was wrong with him. Only Vellard seemed particularly strange here. Perhaps he was going the way of that other officer.

To Ricard's relief Deschaves' return disrupted this train of thought. He repeated his question as the captain laid four tin mugs on the table and poured strong-smelling red wine into each of them.

"About half a mile. Sorry about the 'glasses'."

Ricard almost chuckled and took his mug. Deschaves was making him feel comfortable. The man seemed to have a strong presence. When he spoke his words were often declaimed in a way that felt strangely, reassuringly familiar. He latched onto this comforting feature of the captain and resolved to try and restrain his curiosity about the village and to satisfy the questions in his mind about his new subordinates. He drank quickly from the mug, allowing the bitter smell and taste of the wine temporarily to drown the scent of untreated wood that hung in the air.

The conversation stuttered whenever it turned to Jannert or Vellard, but Deschaves often spoke for them. He gave Ricard a rough account of the conditions in the war. Ricard tried to file this information alongside the desolation he had seen outside. He attempted to relate these facts with what he had seen, and then with his own war. There was a connection between Deschaves' words and the things he had seen, he could grasp that. But the gap between these two things, which themselves remained distinct in his mind, and the quiet days on Grenon remained unbridgeable.

On Grenon there had been long hours of depressing waiting, and there had been disease – dysentery mostly – but there had not been sudden death or the days and nights of watching friends' intestines rot slowly over the parapet of the trench. On Grenon barbed wire had only really been used to keep animals out of the barracks, not for trapping men. On Grenon, where the civilisation of the empire was marked most by the dipping of British colours as they brought food into the bay overgrown with vines, one man had been killed by the struggle with the Kaiser. Here in France where there had been so many empires, everyone had become a victim of the war because everyone, from what Deschaves was saying, was dead, mutilated or bereaved. All the officers had fought at Verdun. On Grenon Ricard had smiled with pride when he had read that Verdun was no longer in danger. It had coincided with his own victory. These men had not even been able to celebrate the Armistice. So they said.

Ricard sat there while his ears absorbed the facts and his mind resisted them. He dared not contradict them though, the triad of faces at the end of the table, but a question bubbled inside him until the pressure of it forced it out of his lips.

"But don't you want to go home? After all this?"

He overrode Deschaves' words and the captain fell silent.

"Go home to what?"

Jannert's question was insubordinate but he was clearly upset. Ricard let it pass and looked at him inquiringly.

"I used to live near Verdun. My father had a tailor's shop there. He was never very successful, but he worked hard at it all his life. It was something. I would have had it. But now I've only got the army. My father is too ill even to think about trying again."

Ricard thought of the miserable eyes in Paris. Then Vellard cleared his throat. They turned to him in surprise.

"Besides, we owe it to them."

"To who?"

He had a similar accent to Deschaves, somewhere near Nice, he thought. Strange that each of them had come so far only to end up together. Ricard sat up expectantly. Surely Vellard must have somewhere to go, and he did not look like a career soldier, a second son like his new major. This was the real reason.

"To them."

He waved a hand hesitantly, seemingly more nervous even than the others about setting off any disturbances in the air.

"Them?"

Deschaves cut in and silenced the lieutenant by placing a hand firmly on his shoulder.

"He means the men who died. Some of the soldiers are a little – superstitious. You will see tomorrow."

Ricard sat back, unsure whether he had failed in his

enquiry. It occurred to him that he knew where he had seen the captain's attitude before. It was at school. Deschaves must have been a teacher. He felt satisfied with himself at spotting this, and even more reassured. Not everything had been upset. A teacher was still a teacher. Suddenly a thought struck him and he nervously made one last venture.

"Is that what – you know – *affected* my predecessor?"

Deschaves shrugged.

"Who knows? We have finished the wine, I'm afraid. Shall I fetch another bottle?"

Ricard thought he read the expression on his face astutely.

"No, no my friends, I should sleep. I have barely slept since I reached Bordeaux. I shall see you all tomorrow. May I request that you, Captain, lead the reveille parade tomorrow? I shall regard you as commander here until I have had chance to read my orders, but I shall expect you to attend me in my quarters following the parade – I would like to know more about this place. Is there anyone to guide me to my quarters?"

Deschaves allowed a half-smile to creep over his face during this speech, but at its conclusion he nodded and spoke quietly to the sentry outside, who hurried off into the wet dark. He returned leading a short, squat figure.

"Sergeant Deloi. He will attend you sir."

"Thank you, Captain. I will see you tomorrow morning."

Ricard nodded to the two lieutenants, who saluted with that same quiet air that he had seen so often as he moved further from Paris.

"Good night sir. Sleep well."

Deschaves smiled as he saluted. Ricard smiled back and went out into the rain. Deloi walked in front of his commander.

"This way sir, I'm afraid that it's not the most wonderful accommodation, sir, but I've put the oil lamp on, sir, so you can see your way around, sir."

The sergeant had no coat. The shoulders of his tunic were soaked and creased as though he had been seized there by huge claws. He wore his helmet to protect his head from the rain, but Ricard could see grey hair beneath its rim.

"I'm sure it will be fine, Sergeant."

"Thank you, sir."

It was another little hut, very much like the one he had just left, except that the smell of cut wood was stronger. It was divided by a long curtain that felt cold. On one side there was a desk, and a chair, and Ricard's trunk. On the other was his bed, a low cold bed, but Ricard decided he would get used to it. There was no point making a fuss. All the men who had served would look at him not with the eyes of Paris, but with contempt. Even Deschaves, the only person who had smiled at him, would share it.

Deloi hung Ricard's coat on the back of the door as though hoping it would dry out, and took away his boots, perhaps to clean them. Ricard sent him away for the night. He wanted to get away from all those subdued movements. He opened his trunk and took out the things he wanted to put on his desk. One was a photograph of a woman in a metal frame. He had bought it from a British officer on Jamaica, who, perhaps, had stolen it from one of his comrades. The woman had long curled hair and stern eyebrows. Ricard did not find her attractive, but it reminded him Grenon. His other link to his quiet war was his journal, which still had sand between its leaves. He picked up the oil lamp and turned to his account of his only few minutes of combat, when a small German ship had nosed towards the bay, inquisitively.

Ricard had mobilised the garrison with a few shouts, and the little ship had been met with four strictly drilled volleys of rifle fire and a shot across the bows from one of the medium-sized guns in the earthworks of the fort. The ship had stopped half in and half out of the bay with the sun shining off its guns and a gentle breeze stirring the ensign where it hung above the bridge. Ricard ordered someone to run up the flag. He looked through his binoculars and felt his heart thump. He could see the bright decks of the ship and a figure on the deck holding its arm and running towards the stern.

He looked along the smart rank of his soldiers, swallowed and told the NCOs to carry on. Another two volleys, and another shell that dented the prow that moved so slowly on the tidal swell. This time the shots were answered. Ricard stood and watched the deck guns jet smoke and heard the yelling of the gun crew as the shells landed noisily.

Ricard swallowed again and thought he was fainting, but the ship *was* getting smaller, going out of the bay, leaving rumpled water in its wake. It steamed away leaving the smell of gunpowder behind it. Ricard had wiped his brow and glanced at the hot sun. This part of the republic had been successfully defended.

The natives had looked incuriously at the full funeral given to the one gunner who had been knocked on the head by a piece of shrapnel. Ricard had struggled with his self-satisfaction as he read the service and for days afterwards while he had tried to hit the right note in the letter to the man's family.

He closed the journal with immense irritation. It all seemed so alien, especially the sun. This cold wet France not only made him a stranger to its own wounds, but also to his own experience. He grunted and dumped the package of orders on the cover of the journal, which now lay on his desk. He opened the flask of water he had found by his bed and swigged at it hoping to get the cloying taste of red wine off his teeth.

Later, he lay on his bed and stared at the opposite wall. There were four holes in it, in the shape of a cross. Must have belonged to the old major, he mused. He had no desire to replace the crucifix, all the more because it had belonged to a man who had gone mad. It reminded him of Vellard.

"Superstition. Hm."

He muttered this before blowing out the lamp and listening to the rain on the iron parts of the roof.

It was still dark and still raining when he woke up. There was little other sound, certainly no voices and no footsteps. Ricard fumbled around in the dark for matches and relit the oil lamp. Its brass stand was still warm to the touch as he carried it over to the pile of his uniform lying on a rickety chair in the corner. He dressed quickly, searching one-handed through his trunk for his clean shirt. Then he pulled back the dividing curtain and went through into the 'office' section of his hut to find his watch. It was very early. He sat on the table and drank some more water, and looked at the package of orders on the table.

He didn't want to read them now. He put on his greatcoat and picked up his clean boots from outside his door. He then stepped out into the cold pre-dawn air. There was no sentry, he noticed. Suddenly he felt unprotected. He was not used to that. The ground was soft underfoot and the air had a tang in it. The turtles again.

The nearest sentry was visible by the glowing tip of a cigarette. Ricard approached him. The soldier heard his footsteps and issued a challenge in a low voice, but relaxed and saluted when Ricard gave his name.

"Good morning sir."

Ricard could just make out his figure against the building he had been appointed to protect. He grunted a reply and moved on, not really knowing where he was going. He sensed that there was more space around him now, and saw low huts, not much bigger than the one he had just left, stretched out in a line to his right. He glanced over his shoulder and saw the sentry crossing himself. The lit end of his cigarette marked the motions of his hand. Ricard could not identify anything else that he recognised, and was afraid of going on. Not that the surroundings frightened him. They seemed to be totally innocuous. Any apprehension, any expectation that Ricard felt about his position, came from within himself. Everything else just sat there, its significance shrouded by the dark. Ricard stepped noisily through the mud back to the sentry.

"Is there anywhere I can get some coffee?"

There was no reply. Ricard repeated his question in a threatening voice with an added "damn you". Still no reply. Ricard reached out and tried to tap the sentry's shoulder. His hand collided with the man sooner than he expected. The sentry was shaking, shaking as though he was thawing from a solid lump of ice. But as Ricard reach out his other hand, he let out an anguished groan, his rifle slipped to the ground and he stood still.

"Are you all right?"

"Oh, sir, did you not feel it?"

The words came out as growls and gasps as though the man was getting his breath back.

"Feel what, man? You've had a fit."

He could see the whites of the sentry's eyes in the very faint light.

"You should report yourself sick. When does your relief arrive?"

"H-half an hour sir."

"Get him now. It's on my authority. Then report

yourself sick."

"I'm not sick, sir. It happens all the time."

"All the more reason for you to report. I can't have men under my command suffering fits on duty. Do it, man."

"Yes sir... you didn't see it, sir?"

"There was nothing to see. You are ill. Do as you are told."

The soldier hurried off, leaving his rifle in the mud. The barrel rested on Ricard's foot. He picked the gun up. He could not go inside until the sentry was replaced. No barracks, no matter how ramshackle, could be treated so casually. He blinked. The lack of a long sleep was catching up with him already. But around him there seemed to be sudden movement. Over in the line of huts he could see lights coming on. In the building behind him he could hear voices and bodies moving around. Ricard was puzzled. It was still early, surely. Time could not have passed so quickly. He blew on his ungloved hands. As he did so a door slammed in the building behind him and figure jogged out, shrugging on a long greatcoat. Ricard challenged him aggressively, disdaining the quietness of other sounds. The figure spun round, raising its hands.

"Lieutenant Jannert, soldier."

The voice trembled. The condescension it attempted failed dismally, particularly in conjunction with the submissively-raised hands.

"What is going on, Lieutenant?"

"Sir? I... I don't know sir. I'm sorry sir."

"That's all right. Why are you running around like that?"

"I'm not sure sir. A bad dream I... I... I hope."

Ricard sighed. No wonder his predecessor had gone mad, he thought, trying to keep control of men like this. Then he thought again of the things Deschaves had told him the night before, and that he had not understood them properly. This was France, not Grenon. He spoke charitably out of his irritation and explained why he was there.

"I'll keep the post, sir, if you like. I don't think I'll sleep again this morning."

"As you wish, Lieutenant. Mind you, I don't think I shall either. I spoke to the sentry about coffee – that's when I noticed what had happened to him. Do you know anything about how to get some?"

Jannert shrugged.

"I don't know sir. I have not had chance to find out yet. Captain Deschaves is awake, though."

"Thank you, Lieutenant."

He handed the rifle to Jannert and went round the side of the building. He saw Deschaves standing at an open door, out of which the light of an oil lamp shone.

"Good morning, Captain."

"Morning sir. You are up rather early."

"As you are. I was looking for some coffee. It has been a rather eventful morning."

"Has it Sir?"

Deschaves spoke quickly. Ricard could not see his face, but he detected nervousness in the hesitation.

"Let's have some coffee and I'll tell you about it."

"Er, yes, yes, sir. We have some here. Do come in. Jacques is awake. I shall go and fetch some hot water."

Ricard stepped into the semi-warmth of the hut. He felt the dampness of the outside slowly evaporating from his hair. Vellard was crouching in the corner, splashing his face in cold water from a bowl. He stood up quickly when Ricard's figure caught his eye. He was in his shirtsleeves, with tousled hair. He saluted slowly.

"I'm sorry, Lieutenant."

Vellard twitched his face, but did not answer. Ricard

studied his eyes, which would not look at him, but flicked from surface to surface in the room. In the discolouring light of the oil lamp they looked red and swollen. Ricard decided not to press the conversation. He stood and looked at the narrow partitions between the three low beds. Curtains concealed them almost entirely. Ricard was curious about what these three berths might reveal about his subordinates, but he did not want to intrude. The only clue for his curiosity was a large book on the table that stood in the middle of a large antechamber. Without looking at the still figure of Vellard, he turned it round with his finger, *Les Miserables*. Ricard tapped his finger on the cover.

"Is this yours, Lieutenant?"

"No, it's mine. You know, I found it in a German trench."

Deschaves' voice was no longer nervous. He walked past Ricard wearing a sardonic grin. He picked up Vellard's jacket with his free hand and watched as the lieutenant struggled into it. Vellard hunched his shoulders as though afraid as soon as his arms were firmly in the sleeves and did not look up at either of his superiors.

"Never had the chance to read it yet. Jacques, I think you and Lieutenant Jannert should take an early parade today. I think the men are… awake, if you see what I mean."

"Sir."

Vellard stumbled out of the hut. Deschaves placed a large dented metal jug on the table. Steam curled slowly from it, and the smell of coffee permeated the stale pipe smoke and damp. Deschaves grinned, carefully.

"I suspect that this is the time that we should discuss Pericard," Ricard began. "Colonel Blamanchard was right – it is a strange place, but I have no doubt that I have just seen a very sick man on sentry duty, and I would like to know why he was there."

Deschaves poured coffee into tin mugs. As Ricard sipped the hot black liquid he thought he could taste red wine in it.

"A sick man, sir?"

Ricard explained what he had seen. Deschaves pursed his lips and looked up from under his eyebrows at his superior.

"I doubt very much, that this man is any sicker than any of the others. With all due respect, those who have served in the war are – different men, sir. Pericard… has an effect on men's minds, sir. May I respectfully request that, before you pursue this matter, you read your orders."

Deschaves smiled wanly under his moustache. Ricard rolled his eyes but had to accept the justice of what the captain had said. He could understand the provincial teacher. No one else had made as much sense since he had come back to France.

"Very well. I shall do that now. Meet me… in an hour and a half. Can I expect some food this morning?"

Deschaves' grin was full now, though Ricard thought he could see sweat on his brow. He frowned but nodded when the captain answered.

"Deloi will attend on you. I shall see to it personally, sir."

Ricard thanked him and rose from the table still clutching his coffee. He went through the door and crossed the mud, which in the growing light was interrupted by scattered patches of ugly grass. There were people about now. He could hear their voices. Women, even children. The villagers of Pericard, returned to miserable wooden huts, he supposed. Then, near his own door, he heard more female tones. They sounded pleading. Then he could hear a male voice. He though it was Deloi.

"The major's not here. I don't know what he'll think

of you coming here so soon. I can't say whether he'll see you today. I think you should go back. He'll be busy. He's only just arrived."

Ricard hurried his steps. He could see three figures standing at the door just outside the throw of the oil lamp's beams. They were shawled against the cold air and their arms were folded. In the doorway itself was Deloi's shape. Ricard felt irritation well up inside him, at the sergeant as much as at the newcomers.

"Sergeant! What do you mean by choosing who I wish to see? Go and get me some breakfast, for God's sake!"

Deloi was immediately apologetic.

"Sorry, sir, right away. I've brought you hot water, sir."

He hurried away. Ricard turned to the three women. Two were young, one old. All three had lined faces and their shawls and hair seemed mingled together with filth and sweat. They had defiant but defeated expressions. They smelt of shit and damp and the mud of eastern France was ingrained in their skins. Ricard ran a hand down his face, suddenly conscious again of his suntan and his neat uniform.

"Captain? – Major?"

This was the tallest of the three. Ricard had forgotten that he had not yet put on his new epaulettes. He nodded politely to her, trying not to look too hard at her chapped and split lips. She parted them again, but Ricard interrupted whatever it was she was about to say.

"I am sorry for my crude language. I am also sorry that my attendant was right. I am unable to speak to you today. As he said – and I am sorry that he did not do so with more grace – I have only just arrived. I have not yet even had chance to read my own orders. I have not seen Pericard in the daylight. But I promise you that if your case is urgent I will hear what you have to say tomorrow morning. Is it urgent?"

He licked his lips nervously. He knew he sounded like a fool. They looked at him as though he was speaking another language. He probably was. The language of Grenon, where the only women were native women, and French women only appeared in *Les Miserables*. But they answered him.

"It is urgent. It is very urgent. Please listen to us."

"I am sorry. If you need food... no doubt my men can help you. Shelter or something? I do not know what to tell you to do."

"Not food, not shelter, not today."

"Then I give you my word of honour – tomorrow morning."

The women nodded deferentially to him, but did not move. They did not speak again and watched him as he edged round them. He did know what else to do. They just stared at him, the crucifixes round their necks beginning to reflect the dawn's pale light. He closed the door behind him and leaned against it as though he had been chased into his hut. He opened his eyes and saw the chipped pottery bowl on his desk alongside the orders and journal, which had been moved thoughtfully aside.

He splashed the hot water over his head and dried his eyes on the flannel so that he could see the green leaf patterns on the edge. Ricard put the bowl on the floor and pushed his orders in front of him again. He looked at the package for a few seconds, unwilling to open it because it would give him full responsibility over this difficult place. He was hungry and the package looked intimidating.

He sighed and ripped open the seals. The major's epaulettes fell out onto the table. He brushed them aside and returned to the orders. They were typed on thin, flimsy paper with occasional crossings-out where the copyist had missed a key. He flipped through them without enthusiasm, and noticed that large sections were underlined in red ink.

He scratched his unshaven chin and separated the more general orders, including the confirmation of his promotion, which he would read over and savour later, from the more specific ones. These were where most of the red underlining was.

At the moment he began reading Deloi knocked on the door and brought in breakfast – some meat and bread, and more coffee. He was still apologetic but Ricard sent him back through the door with an irritated snap. Ricard bent his eyes to the page again while he chewed absently on his food. He had to concentrate on the underlined sections now, he decided. Deschaves would be coming soon, and he still had to send a message back to Blamanchard saying that he had arrived and was in charge.

By the time Deschaves knocked on the door he was beginning to feel as though he was gaining some grasp of the situation. He had a means now for understanding Pericard, and, in a way, France as a whole. Orders made the whole thing feel structured. The landscape he had seen outside was a mess, but now he had an approach that would help him clear it up. He had practically memorised the underlined sections by the time he followed Deschaves out of the door and left instructions for a message to be relayed to Colonel Blamanchard.

"…3b. You must take exceptional care in the removal of bodies from the battlefield and the temporary battlefield cemeteries, and during the process of identification of the bodies, that no persons attempt to take any of these bodies from the immediate vicinity of Pericard without direct permission. This permission must only be granted if there is an official warrant presented to you. If you are in any doubt, seek confirmation from Regimental HQ in Rheims. However, in pursuit of this aim do not alienate those who seek to remove the bodies. This is counter-productive. Beware of attempts to remove bodies surreptitiously…

"Additional: This must only be discussed with Captain Henri Deschaves, who has been in acting command since the indisposition of Major Le Blanc.

"Reports have been received of a growth of mental illness amongst veterans serving at Pericard which has been combined with an upsurge in religious fervour. It has been suggested that such a combination is detrimental to the discipline of the Army and may also have political ramifications. You are instructed to observe any phenomena of this nature and report to Major Desailles at Rheims. You are only to discuss these phenomena with Major Desailles and Captain Deschaves…"

Ricard had pulled this sheet from the pile of orders to study it further. It was typed on different, thicker paper. There were no mistakes. He handed it to Deschaves as they stepped out of the hut. The captain had only glanced at it before Ricard spoke, suddenly thinking of other questions.

"Why is there no sentry outside my quarters? There might be more of these women."

The three of them still stood there in the growing light, which made them look even dirtier and even more miserable. He could guess now why they were there. He hoped they had warrants. He did not like carrying out harsh orders, but he would carry them out if he had to.

"I'm sorry sir. The men did not like seeing one there – or serving there – after your predecessor was indisposed."

"I am not my predecessor. But thank you for arranging my breakfast."

"My pleasure sir. I will arrange for a sentry to be posted."

Deschaves' feet knew where he was going already, since his eyes were already skipping over the text of "Additional". Ricard walked alongside him, looking ahead to where two or three soldiers were standing either side of the flattened mud of the track. They saluted the two officers with the exaggerated slowness that Ricard had come to expect. Even Deschaves had it in his walk. All the soldiers had rifles slung across their chests, and he could see mud in the barrels. Ricard mentally noted this down. A little further along he could see barbed wire laid along either side of the track, and beyond it, just wasteland.

"Captain?"

"Yes sir?"

"How far are we from the front line?"

"Still the same as last night, sir. About half a mile. There are communication trenches on either side of us. They go back beyond the present village. On the right was a gun battery."

Ricard swivelled his eyes.

"I can't see it."

It looked more featureless than a stormy Atlantic, and the smell that was almost like the turtles was much stronger here. He swallowed some of the stale air and looked down to where inches of mud had congealed around his boots and dirtied the lower parts of his uniform. He could feel the mud creeping up him.

"I'll show you sir. Be careful. There is a lot of material still not cleared up."

Ricard followed in Deschaves' path, tripping occasionally over stones, pieces of metal, wood, wire and skirting with the captain cavernous dents or excavations in the uneven ground. Ricard shuddered as his eyes, getting used to seeing the distinctive features of the chaos, picked out scattered effects of soldiers – weapons, boots, helmets, even clothing – at the bottom of these holes. They lay in between fragments of metal. He swallowed. The smell of the turtles welled up in his nose and he began to comprehend what it meant. He tried, and succeeded – just – to keep his voice level as he spoke loudly towards where Deschaves' back was framed against the grey sky.

"Is it safe, out here?"

"Not… exactly sir. It is very difficult to make sure that we have removed as yet unexploded shells from everywhere."

"How much ground is officially clear?"

"Half a square mile, sir. And even that is being generous."

Ricard almost stopped in astonishment.

"They've given me twenty square miles to clear! By Christmas!"

Deschaves looked over his shoulder just as splashes of rain began to drop as tentatively as he and the other soldiers moved. He had a wry smile on his face.

"Don't worry sir. They gave the old major the same task. And that was in November."

Ricard wasn't entirely reassured by this, but by that point they had reached what remained of the battery. There were a few decaying sandbags and thousands of caps from shells. And messages. Bits of paper, some formal, some torn from notebooks, some soaked to an ugly pulp by the rain. Most were smeared and largely illegible. Ricard crouched down to examine one of them, and gleaming metal seemed to spring into his vision. Crucifixes, images of Mary the Virgin, rosaries, empty crosses, rings, lockets and some items he could not identify but which he presumed were put there by men of other religions, or perhaps had some personal significance. With a careful hand he stilled the fluttering of one piece of paper which, it seemed, had been torn roughly from some printed book. The left half of the writing, written in blue ink, sloping upwards as it went into a mass of smudges, could still be read: "O holy… the soul of… my only… Somme, 1917". He looked at others. Where they were not obscured, they all carried similar messages. Some were written in Latin, others in a script that he could not read – he thought it might be Hebrew. He heard Deschaves taking the "Additional" out of his pocket. He knew it was that. There could be nothing else, he knew, unless he had his own message to add to the shrine. Ricard stared for a few more seconds at the hundreds, perhaps thousands of tokens and stood, and turned to Deschaves. The captain handed him the "Additional".

"Why here?"

"Not just here, sir. The front line trenches – what's left of them – sometimes have the same things in them."

"You'd better show me. You can also explain to me what is going on."

Deschaves surveyed him with a kind of satisfied expression, as though this was a carefully planned surprise. He did not answer immediately, and they started walking deeper into the battlefield. Ricard's shudders signalled to him how his body was reacting to this mass expression of faith. Religion vaguely alarmed him as it was, but to find it here, where it did not look as though civilised men had visited since the beginning of time, left him completely bewildered. The sounds of the village reached them faintly over the stinking chaos. Ricard, with his back to it, felt as though he was walking from an alien world into a void. Despite the presence of Deschaves he felt alone. Even the wisps of his breath in the cold air appeared to be abandoning him.

"Did you ever hear, sir, of a place called Bois-Brule?"

The captain's voice was so low that even coming unexpectedly as it did, it did not frighten him.

"Yes. I think I read about it during the war. The dead answering from the ground, and helping our men defeat the Boches. An interesting story."

"There are other stories like it sir."

"And I presume that there is some such myth here at Pericard."

"I – are you all right, sir?"

"Yes, yes."

"Are you sure, sir?"

"Yes. I have seen dead men before. I... I have seen them. I was surprised. He looks like the ground."

"He has probably been under it for some time, sir. Sometimes they do emerge like that."

"How?"

"I don't know, sir. I am told it happens everywhere. Do you want to go back?"

"No, no. Where are the trenches?"

"Just over there, sir. If you would like to carry on, I will mark the place where he lies."

As Ricard stumbled forward around the body, he felt his thoughts rush back into his head from wherever they had hidden themselves. The dead gunner on Grenon, the men, the natives dead from disease or accidents – they had never been left to rot like that, so long that the bones and the uniform seemed fused and the rifle with its bayonet still attached appeared to have grown like some unnatural plant through the ribs. Barbed wire snatched at his legs. He lowered his eyes to it, glad to get them away from contemplation of this unending plain of filth. As he glanced down the smell increased and he dared not look up again for fear of confronting more bones wriggling off the earth from their graves and accosting him.

He looked behind him where it was safe, and saw Deschaves just raising his head from what looked like a still pose, and removing his hands from behind his back. He was glad to see that the captain too gave the dead man a wide berth. As he approached, Ricard could see a slightly distant look in his eyes.

"Be careful as you get near to the edge, sir."

His mouth moved almost mechanically. Ricard shuddered. He took a few more steps and the line of the trench became visible stretching away, a continuous fissure in the fabric of the mud.

"The actual front line and advance trenches are some way on the other side of this one. This is where the dugouts used to be. I think they've fallen in now."

Ricard surveyed the pit in front of him. On the other side there was a broken line of sandbags. Beyond that, two stuttering parallels marked the real front line. Then there was no man's land, where the ground was churned so much it barely looked solid. Ricard tried to imagine a night here, and dared not.

"The trenches are filling up with silt."

Deschaves was speaking quickly. Ricard wasn't sure why. Perhaps it was to do with the dead man, perhaps with his own questions. Either way, he did not interrupt by repeating them.

"Ultimately, we want this to happen, but not just yet. There are dead men in there, and other things that we want to retrieve."

"Have you not yet cleared the dead? How many have you retrieved?"

"More than you would think. And there are still many more."

His eyes were distant again. To shorten the time he must spend out here, Ricard raised the "Additional" that Deschaves had put into his hand. Deschaves registered it after a few seconds and pointed to where a narrow channel ran at right angles towards the frontline sandbags.

"Look in the communications trench."

Ricard moved forwards and crouched to look along the trench. He froze as he saw what was in there. Every few feet there was a rifle thrust barrel-first into the earth, and a helmet balanced on the part of it that emerged from the ground. Rifle, helmet, rifle, helmet… the pattern led away along the silted ground so far as the curvature of the walls would let him see. The memorials, for he was aware that that was what they were, were not uniform. Some were set lower in the ground than others, perhaps put there in memory of particular men before new layers of earth began to overwhelm them. The men's memories were protected from the wind, and some of the rain, but the earth was still rising around them. Ricard could not even hear his own breathing. He gazed for too long, his brain told him. He closed his eyes and breathed in the foetid air. He did not look at the helmets, but up and away from them to find Deschaves. He could not see him.

"Captain Deschaves!"

The noise seemed to reverberate even though it could not. Ricard had a strange feeling that even the village could hear him, and that they would all pause in their soft movements to hear this loud new officer. After a few seconds, Deschaves replied. He appeared on the other side of the trench, revolver in hand, breathing heavily.

"Sorry sir. A rat. I don't like rats."

"Captain, I am fascinated by what's here, but I should see what else there is for me to do in Pericard."

Deschaves nodded He took a long run up and leapt over the trench, sending little wreaths of mud from his boots spiralling into it. He smiled apologetically to Ricard.

"I could not have done that a few months ago, sir."

"You would have been killed?"

"No, the trench would have been wider. If we had so much raised our heads here during the war, we would have joined the dead. There was a machine gun aimed at the communication trench. There are more messages where it used to be."

Ricard fell silent. His mind and his reflexes had always saved him from danger before, but here he would have been no luckier than the stupidest and slowest soldier. He found it almost impossible to imagine a situation in which there was no escape except through an unlikely chance. A cold feeling told him that he would have died in the war if he had been there, even though clearly slow-witted men like Deloi had survived.

Only the moments since the trenches remained clear in Ricard's mind as he sat at his desk that evening. He was struggling to write a report of the day's events to Colonel Blamanchard. The report for Major Desailles had already been completed. It was brief and factual: "…it is a waste of time for me to speculate at the moment, since I have only just arrived…" This report had been sealed and despatched. He hoped there would be a quick reply, to offer him more guidance. Even the most basic things about this effusion of faith confused him. The sites seemed to be completely non-denominational, a feature with which he was unfamiliar. Were they for luck, or protection, or just a mark of respect for the men whose bodies were still out in no man's land? He decided to listen to his own words in the completed report, to stop speculating and get on with the one still as yet incomplete.

He could remember the afternoon parade he had ordered. He had wandered up and down between ranks of soldiers whose shoulders slumped even when they were at attention. They were in a shocking state, but he could not bring himself to be angry with them. The parade was conducted in the middle of the village amidst the noises of hammering from villagers working on their huts, of children playing in the mud and making themselves almost as filthy as the skins of the soldiers.

He could not remember the structure of the organisation which had arranged the setting up of the temporary homes with white numbers painted on the loose-hinged doors though he knew he understood it, as he understood the apportioning of men to the old battlefields, what they did there with their carts and patient horses, where the bodies, German and French, were laid when they were found, and how and where they were buried. He knew he understood it all, but it was so hard to put on paper. His understanding was too compressed into a small space surrounded by a lack of knowledge.

He sat and twiddled his pen and thought about the memorials in the trenches in their silence. He tried to recall his words to the scruffy soldiers about the need for a professional appearance again. He tried to picture in detail the tarpaulin under which the decaying corpses were laid until they were identified or buried. He looked down at the five lines he had typed on the heavy machine. He stood up and stalked out of the hut into the early evening rain.

Celine

She could see the new major clearly as he left the parade ground. Behind him the soldiers were falling out in order to go on with their duties, to go out onto the battlefield and carry more bodies back.

All the moving figures except this one, the major's, were indistinct, as usual. No other bodies were between the two of them. It was as though, as Lieutenant Vellard had said, this man who had not been here before had killed the dead again. The mist that shrouded everything else in her perception did not touch him.

"He does not understand."

Lieutenant Vellard's eyes had been wide, and his voice, though reduced to a whisper, was forceful.

"Of course he doesn't. In five years' time there will be millions who do not understand. It's only we who will ever understand."

"But if he doesn't he will do as he is told, he will destroy the battlefields and then – what will they have died for?"

She had seen desperation in the lieutenant, but she had no ready answer. He had caught her arm, unsuspected, in the very early mists of morning before the parade had begun. She was not especially close to Lieutenant Vellard, but everyone in Pericard shared the experiences. She had just happened to be passing him as his doubts had burst out of him. The dead ones had not been seen that night, and Lieutenant Vellard was afraid that the new major had driven them away. She was not convinced, and in any case she had a material issue to discuss and she was not at all upset to discover that she was to discuss it with a man who was only interested in material things.

The major had seen her now, and was looking at her intently as she stood with Marie and Anne outside his hut. She could see his thick build, darkened face and neat clothing more clearly from a distance that she had seen Lieutenant Vellard's face close to. Lieutenant Vellard had been obscured by the confusion which had gathered around him like thick glass, but the major was as well-defined as the crucifix she clutched at her neck. After a few moments he reached them and took off his officer's cap. He spoke very formally, as though he was regimenting the sounds in his mouth.

"Good morning. I am sorry to have kept you waiting. Come in, please."

The sentry at his door saluted as they entered. She half-smiled at him; she knew him and she knew that he was glad to be there. He was almost frightened about going out to the trenches today. They all had a feeling about going to the trenches today.

That, she had to admit, was something that had been affected by the coming of the new major. He had dragged Private Mareille from them while the dead were still speaking, before they had said what they wanted to say. Everyone in the village had felt the major's hand on their shoulder. The dead had retreated in disorder while the major shook the poor sentry back into life. The trenches were dangerous – that was all they knew, and the dead had chosen not to speak again.

In the hut she could smell the major, his cigarettes, his breakfast, his sweat, and even the damp that came from the walls. She could tell that Anne and Marie could smell him too, and that they were surprised. It was rare to smell a living person. The major was unaware of all this. He pointed to three chairs arranged in front of his desk.

"Please sit down. I will not stand on military discipline for once. I am sorry that the seats are not more comfortable, but Captain Deschaves tells me they are the best he can find."

He smiled with friendly eyes at them. She saw it as a signal from the other side of a long bridge. They had not yet replied to him, and she could see that this made him uncomfortable. His speech began to flounder.

"Sergeant Deloi will bring coffee soon – I hope that you will all join me in a mug or two."

"Yes, that would be very nice."

She said it woodenly, but sat at the same time. Marie and Anne copied her. The major took his own seat on the other side of the desk. His hand flicked through sheets of blank paper. For a moment there was no conversation. She could see Anne pursing her wrinkled lips and knew she was worried about the trenches. The trenches were immediate. They had already been waiting a long time for what they were to ask from the major.

He broke the silence by clearing his throat.

"I think I can guess why you have come to me. I want you to understand that I know you might be suspicious of me. You've come to take bodies away, back to your homes, I think. Am I right?"

He looked at them almost nervously. Celine's eyes held some sort of attraction for him, and he could not look away for long. She did not look away and she did not reply. There was a pause.

"Yes. But we aren't suspicious of you, are we?"

Marie's voice was high and didn't seem to issue from her grimy throat. The major nodded.

"I think I should make my official position clear. I am only allowed to release those remains which have been firmly identified and for which there is an authorised warrant. All others – well, I expect that you will have seen the cemetery that is being created. It will be an honourable resting-place, I can assure you."

Celine spoke loudly, to forestall Anne's protest.

"We appreciate that sir. But…"

"I understand. Tell me, have you applied for warrants? I must warn you that any attempt to remove the bodies through non-official channels will be severely punished."

For all his firmness, it felt as though he was uttering his statements from a half-learned script.

Celine lowered her eyes as she suspected he had wanted her to do earlier. She felt ashamed of her interest in the way he gazed at her.

"No, I'm sorry, we haven't applied for warrants."

"I will do it for you, if you wish."

This startled her. She had lived for so long with the desires of others already known to her that this, coming from nowhere that she recognised, astonished her. She was instantly, surgingly grateful and she could feel warmth flooding out from herself and the others. He went on speaking.

"I shall have to see you all separately of course, in order to find out the facts of each case. The adjudicators will want to know all relevant details. Are there any others besides yourselves who need warrants?"

"Some, sir."

She kept her eyes lowered. The major pulled the sheets of blank paper towards him and took up a pencil. His movements were noisy and she could see how hard he gripped the edge of the first page.

"Please tell me your names, and the names of the men you want to recover, and the names of the other 'some'."

It was a moment before she realised, by the glint in his eyes, that this was an attempt at humour. But by this time Deloi had tiptoed into the room and deposited a tray on the table. She could smell the heat of the coffee. Deloi was afraid, but the major didn't notice. He simply instructed him to bring some water in half an hour's time. Deloi left without speaking and the major poured the coffee into the mugs. The women drank, but barely tasted it. The major looked at them again.

"I will do the administrative work for you, but on one condition. You must answer all my questions truthfully. All of them, even if they seem irrelevant. One good turn deserves another. Is that a fair exchange?"

They did not answer but he appeared to take this as assent. She could feel Anne's consternation, but the old woman was pleased as well. It was she who gave her name first.

"Anne Lamarque. I… I want to take my son home. His name is… Francois. He is, was, a private soldier in the Hundred and thirty-eighth regiment."

The major did not remark on her use of the present tense.

"Marie Teroux. My brother – a sergeant of the same regiment."

Marie almost collapsed into tears. The major turned to his third visitor.

"I am Celine Delain. I am here for my husband of the Hundred and fifty-third. Lieutenant Jean-Paul Delain."

The major put down his pencil.

"You are an officer's wife? How interesting. I did not expect that after, after…"

He waved his arm feebly in the direction of the other two women. Celine found herself meeting his gaze again.

"The war changed my life as much as it changed theirs, sir."

The major put his head in his hands. Hesitantly the women gave the names and dead men of the other four women who had managed to make their way across France to Pericard. He wrote them down with much less resolution in his movements. At last he raised his head and spoke briskly.

"Very well. I will see as many of you as I can this afternoon. I have orders to write this morning, and I also have to go out to the trenches to observe the work in progress."

"Please don't go out to the trenches sir. It's dangerous."

Anne could not restrain herself. Celine tried to calm her with a hand on her arm. She was very agitated. But the major smiled, undisturbed.

"I went out there yesterday. Do not be concerned about me. I know what it's like."

"But it'll be different today sir."

At that moment Celine felt her husband's hand on her shoulder. She jumped to her feet, knowing that Marie's hand was on her rosary and Anne's was on her heart. She didn't feel the coffee she spilt on her legs.

"What is it? What's going on?"

The major's face was horrified but uncomprehending. She stared at him while her husband told her what had happened. An unexploded shell had gone off and taken with it a young soldier's hand. With the breaking of silence on the battlefield the armistice on men's lives had also been broken. Another memorial would have to be made. She did not answer the major's question but bolted from the room towards the track that led to the trenches. Around her she felt other people becoming aware of the event, as dead men told them that their ranks would be swollen.

Jean-Paul's life was leaving him. The shell had done its belated work well. Celine crouched by the improvised bed of sacks under the tarpaulin on the edge of the village feeling all of its prayers flow through her lips. Jean-Paul's face hovered between fear and peace as the blood seeped through the bandage on his hand. He knew that the pain

49

would end soon and he would join the community still lurking in the trenches. He had, in his mind, already said goodbye to his parents and his tuberculous younger sister. He had been planning to look after them with his Army pay, but now he had bequeathed, in whispers, everything he had left to them. That included his body. Celine had new hopes that his wish would be granted.

He was too weak to try and remove the bandage that covered his wound. The bandage was a concession to the outsider, who had insisted that the regimental doctor, Lieutenant Georges, was summoned to tend the injury once the boy had been carried from the old no man's land. His lack of understanding had been accompanied by tears that had alarmed the living and the dead so much that they had given way.

"There's no point in bandaging a dead man, sir."

"He's not dead! I order you to save him!"

At last, when Lieutenant Georges had gone through the motions and Jean-Paul had been made comfortable in the crude hospital building, the major had gone away to write his orders and arrange for the erasure of part of the battlefield. After a tense period of waiting the villagers had slipped their hands under the dying soldier's limbs and taken him to join the mortal remains of his future companions. When they had left Celine had volunteered to stay with him.

Jean-Paul's face was as pale as the skin that still adhered to some of the bones around him.

"My husband will look after you there. He has the same name as you. He came to tell me about what had happened to you."

"Thank you."

It was a painful gasp.

"Ask him to come and see me. He's not visited me properly for such a long time. I hope he isn't angry. I'm

50

trying to do what he wants. Please tell him, won't you?"

"Yes."

The prayers of the village forced themselves back through her lips. When they stopped again the boy was dead. Celine got to her feet, her duty done. It was strange that everyone still feared death here even though it did not mean separation or oblivion or hell. The tarpaulin was a good intermediate point to bring the dying to, since the living and the dead were always present there. The living did a lot of learning under its cover. She had turned to go before she felt the presence of Lieutenant Vellard and his frightened anger.

"What's wrong? Have you come to bury him and the others?"

"The major will not allow it, not as Private Dessons wished, but a military one, we have instructions from him."

He pointed at the newly-dead body.

"Major Villier's going to destroy everything! The battlefields will be gone, the men will be reduced to soldiers' corpses, even now they are frightened and hide out there and don't come to us. The new lieutenant has not been spoken to by them, and he's still afraid!"

Celine did not answer immediately. She knew he spoke for many who were overwhelmed by what they experienced in past and present and had no thoughts left for the future when men like the major would be the majority in Pericard.

"He's doing what has to be done in the end. But…"

She fended off his interruption with a raised hand.

"But I will speak to him. Perhaps he can be brought to understand."

"Understand! What has he lost, what can he know about the war? How can you, of all people, trust him?"

Celine hesitated before answering, but then Captain Deschaves broke into the argument by moving aside the canvas curtain that shielded the bodies from the weather. He snapped his words hurriedly.

"Enough! He's coming over this way. You and I, Jacques, must talk to Jean about the things he'll have started seeing. You're right, Madame Delain. Maybe it is worth speaking to him."

He led the young lieutenant away and his figure was replaced by those of men who had come to bury or re-bury the fallen. She left them struggling with stretchers and wandered in the general direction of the battlefield wondering about Captain Deschaves. There was always something more intense in what he felt when Lieutenant Vellard was nearby, but she could not grasp what it was. The younger officer's thoughts changed in similar moments, but again in a way that could not easily be defined.

She wondered what they had shared in their past, in the war perhaps... Or perhaps earlier. It was strange that no-one in the village could penetrate the veil that hung around them.

But Captain Deschaves was a bigger enigma than simply that strange flicker caused by Lieutenant Vellard. He had never allowed any hint concerning what he felt at heart about clearing the battlefield or the new major to escape him. She could sense his immediate emotions, like his irritation a moment ago, but no-one had ever been able to reach what went on below that. Perhaps this aloofness had allowed his to get on well with the man whom no-one could really contact at all, who had not lost anything in the trenches, as Lieutenant Vellard had said.

"Madame Delain?"

She turned, startled. The major was such a gap in her consciousness that even his feet in the mud seemed to make no sound.

"I'm sorry sir. You startled me."

"Have you anything out there? A... token or something like that."

He pointed in the direction she had been looking, out towards the trenches. She looked full into his face, but then realised that she had not answered.

"Don't forget my condition. All questions that I ask you."

"Yes, I do have a token out there. For my husband."

He pursed his lips and then shook his head uncomprehendingly.

"Please do not take offence at what I say. I am sorry for your husband's death, I assure you, but I can understand why he died. Such things are expected – in a way – in a war. You know what I mean. But the death today – we aren't at war any more, but I've still got to write a letter to his parents... Do you understand?"

He fell silent. His ability to speak, stripped of its formal phrasing, seemed to have exhausted itself.

"I think I understand you, but I don't understand why you're telling it to me. For me, the death of Private Dessons makes more sense than my husband's did at the time."

The major stared at her with a blank face. She frowned, suddenly eager to talk openly to him. But he spoke first.

"Has everyone got a message out there?"

"Everyone who has lost something, someone, yes. But I don't want to go on while we're standing here. I think we should go back to the village to finish what we were talking about this morning."

There were ripples of alarm in the awareness all around her as people began to sense something of the road she was taking. But from the dead she could feel encouragement. The major wore an expression of mild surprise. She wasn't sure why she was so certain that he would grasp what she would tell him, but then, she reasoned, he had wanted to help her. He nodded slowly as though he knew what she was thinking, but then spoke what was really on his mind.

"Instead, take me to your quarters. I can guess from your clothes that they are not all that pleasant. I think your material needs, and those of your companions, should be attended to before those of the dead, who cannot feel. Don't protest. Just show me."

She felt icy at his insistence. She had not truly comprehended how little he understood. Perhaps she was wrong about him after all. But then she had to talk about the burial of Private Dessons. She wanted him to hear the desires of the man himself, so as not to thrust an anonymous military grave upon him, no matter how honourable it was said to be. She would have to pretend to take his path for a while and hope he would listen again soon.

"As you wish sir. Please follow me."

She led him along the rows of iron and wood that made up the new village of the returned refugees. At the furthest point along the road to Rheims that could still be said to be port of the village, she stopped and broke her silence. There, in two crude tents made out of rotten canvas and poles left over from the construction of the houses, lived the women who had come back for their men's remains.

"There, sir."

He went forward and, apologising to the faces that peered out of the stinking interiors, examined the feeble attempts at a fire over which they had warmed some salted meat and the fraying ropes that held the corners of the tents down but did not prevent the wind from blowing under the bedraggled skirts of the canvas onto the emaciated ankles inside. She followed him with her eyes, noticing these details as though for the first time. The other women went back inside after a few moments and lay down on the mud. The only thing they wanted the major to notice was the task they had been set in Pericard of bringing the bodies home. Celine herself was interested in his concern. It was so alien to the things she was concerned with. When he came back to her he was pale and his voice was angry.

"I will have my men build you somewhere to live. There will be no work on the battlefield if necessary until this work is done. Human beings cannot live like this!"

She felt the amusement of nearby veterans at his words, but she remained serious. He was trying to help.

"It's really not that important sir. If would could talk to you about our husbands and brothers coming home – that's what's important."

"Will you not be a woman, and decent, and dry, and clean?"

"I would, but what I came here to do is more important. I'm sorry, I keep telling you, but it is…"

She clutched at the crucifix at her neck and immediately felt faint. In the awareness round her there was an enormous upsurge of mutinous feeling. She could not feel its source but it lapped round the general unity she had grown used to in the village.

"Are you all right?"

The mutiny was growing in strength.

"Sir – please don't bury Private Dessons in the cemetery this afternoon."

"Why not?"

"He didn't wish it – he didn't want it like that."

"What do you mean? God, woman, sit down!"

She felt his hands on her shoulders and she found herself on a rough piece of wood with the major looking down at her. His face turned black and yellow as her vision went faint. She slipped into a dark well filled with the face of her husband smiling seriously as he had smiled in the long summer before the war.

The sun was setting. She sat in the kitchen, smelling what she had prepared for dinner as it heated slowly in the oven. It was warm and the air was thick with summer. She lay back in the chair and felt its sharp back dig into the skin under her shoulder blades. She heard him come into the house and shivered slightly as she felt his hand run up her arm. It was this moment she waited for all day. Even when she was busy in the house, or occupied with the children she taught at the school, in the back of her mind there was always something waiting, a part of her that existed purely to feel those fingers creep up the muscles of her arm to her neck where her flesh would tingle and excited coldness would run down her back. She smiled up into his kiss. After a few moments he stepped back and let his hands fall from her body, leaving cool patches that begged to be heated by him again. His face was serious.

"It looks like war."

"Don't worry about it. Go and get changed. I'll put your dinner out."

His fingers slipped over her forehead. She smiled at him again and he blushed as though he was still the boy she had set her cap at.

"I love you."

"I love you too. Go and get ready."

She awoke to the sound of gunfire rattling out over the grey fields. It faded into silence. Afterwards there were a few seconds of peace before the sensations of the village floated back into her groggy thoughts. The crackle of the rifles had startled her, but her body was heavy and her mind was slow. She realised she must have heard the volleys over a new military grave. She lay where she was and stared up at the dark iron of the roof's underside, feeling the mutiny grow and recede like waves breaking against the background of more familiar feelings. She waited for a long time before the distinctive presence of Captain Deschaves entered the building in which she lay.

"The major has buried him."

"I thought he had. People aren't happy about it, are they?"

"I didn't realise you were so sensitive to it."

Captain Deschaves towered over her. She did not shift her position on the bed to look at him because the frustration he felt was self-evident.

"Lieutenant Vellard refused to attend the funeral. Major Villier says he's ill."

His voice shook. Celine sensed that mysterious flicker again.

"The major's new here. I'm sure he'll become more understanding the longer he stays and he realises that we're all 'ill'. Have you spoken to Lieutenant Jannert?"

"He knows, but he is still afraid. They still smell of the trenches to him."

"Don't they to you? I thought that was how they announced themselves to everyone."

"Yes, yes, but he is still not used to it. Major Villier…"

He stopped. She lay with her eyes directed upwards, feeling the sudden conflicts within the captain. After a moment he went on.

"I don't think Major Villier will come to accept what's going on here."

There was something still in him that wanted to be said, about the major and what he was to do in Pericard.

"Why not?"

He rustled some paper in his pocket.

"I don't. That's all. Anyway, I didn't come to talk

about him particularly, but about where you are to live."

"On his orders?"

"He is the commanding officer. You and your 'companions' will be given a hut the same as those the villagers have."

"He's a good man, you know. He was really upset by what happened to Private Dessons. You saw he was."

The captain closed his mind up suddenly. Celine held back from defending the major further. It was a relief. She was beginning to be afraid that people might begin to notice that she kept taking his side. Captain Deschaves seemed oblivious, however.

"I'm not going to interfere. You understand better than I do. Do as you see fit."

He left. Celine closed her eyes. She saw her husband and the dead private. The smell of the trenches wafted over her and in her ears the sound of their lumbering steps was loud. She could see the familiar pattern of dirt on her husband's face and the caked blood on his tunic and on his hands where he had clutched the wound in a vain attempt to stop his life spraying out of the hole in his chest. It still pained her to see what he had become in death after what he had been in life. He rolled the whites of his eyes until the pupils became visible, and reached out a hand pocked about the wrist with louse bites to touch her face tenderly. Private Dessons looked away from the intimate moment.

"The major's a hope, Jean-Paul. He might let me take you home. And the others might go home. That'd be seven of you at rest. You'll be able to leave the trenches altogether at last. It will happen. And, Private, you know that Lieutenant Vellard will write to your family don't you?"

But Jean-Paul had not come in anger. He wasn't angry with his wife – he was worried for her. But – the major was going to have to be careful. He wasn't to be allowed to act

58

too quickly.

"What? Jean-Paul, you know that this can't last forever. If I don't take you home one day the trenches will be filled in. The major's all part of that. Even I will have to leave eventually."

Jean-Paul dropped his hand from her. He frowned. He said that only here, in Pericard, did the dead men have some chance to make a claim on that which they had lost. Only here was justice possible and he looked to his wife to give his death some sort of meaning. She had to take him home. She had to let him live for as long as he would have lived if it hadn't been for the war.

She nodded eventually and took his hand, feeling the roughness of dirt on it.

"But the injustice will come, won't it? One day no-one will remember. Everyone will be just like the major. They'll be sad for you, but they'll only be imagining. No-one will be able to share the loss once we're gone. They'll put up memorials, but they won't really remember. We can only make it good in our lifetimes. I'm trying to do that for you, but the end must come one day."

Jean-Paul nodded slowly. She mustn't worry too much, not while she was ill. They would talk about it another time. Then he said, almost clearly and audibly:

"Captain Deschaves' brother was a desk major." Celine looked at him questioningly but his hand had slipped out of hers and she could see him walking with his young attendant out of the building. The stench of their presence faded quickly and she was alone in the hut with the beginnings of tears painful in the back of her throat.

Ricard

It had become quite a cold night and the rain was falling steadily, but Ricard did not mind. He dismounted from his horse and gave the reins to the man who had accompanied him.

"I'll walk the rest of the way."

The man nodded and went on ahead. As the clopping of hooves faded Ricard looked around him with a feeling almost like wonder. Rheims at night offered a very different prospect from that of Pericard. It was even unlike itself, hugely different from the way he remembered it from his first visit. Electric lights gleamed in many places, though their illumination often flickered. The reflections they cast sent up spiralling patterns from the wet hard ground, the stone that jarred, unfamiliar, against Ricard's boots. Last time he had been here he had been beginning his journey into the war. Now it felt that he had escaped its grim hold, even if only for a moment. In Rheims life was beginning again. It bustled up against him with pretty female faces and the smell of cigars and perfume. People walked around at night and voices were raised in bright tones from cafes, restaurants and bars. Such establishments had not yet returned to Pericard.

Ricard walked up and down in the cool rain for a long time, his head bared. The signs of war were still evident everywhere but it was refreshing to see that something was beginning to overlay them. After all, that was the process he was trying to begin in Pericard. That night he retired to his barrack-bed – how warm and comfortable! – glowing with the inspiration of Rheims' healing streets. As he dozed into deep sleep the verbal reports he had travelled all this way to make at Colonel Blamanchard's personal request seemed nothing but a formality. Next morning he would speak, they would answer, life would spread back through ruined France and all would be well. It would be that easy to lessen the miserable weight of the past. He could take a little bottle of Rheims' air back with him which would quickly dispel the gloom of all those faces hanging over the dead like morose carvings.

Next morning he was less than pleased to be disillusioned. He was to be questioned with a seriousness that even in his vainer moments he had not known he merited. It seemed that the Army, in the person of the man who faced him, was very concerned about what had happened in Pericard. Major Desailles was a hard-faced man with cheeks like corrugated iron. His thinning hair seemed to be lashed to the top of his head. His voice sounded as though he was crushing chalk between his teeth.

"What do you mean 'you will not speculate on what you have observed?' *That* is what you were *appointed* to do."

Ricard was becoming increasingly irritated by the man's blue stare and his apparent inability to grasp plain French, whether written or spoken. He thought without pleasure of Colonel Blamanchard's comment that the two of them were similar in some ways. He appreciated Desailles' professional approach to military matters, but he hoped that he, Ricard, would never turn into anything this infuriating.

"I did not say that. Sir – are you actually listening to me? I said, I did not feel I was ready to speculate on a situation I knew absolutely nothing about."

"Are you *still* in that position? If so, then we might

have to reconsider your promotion, *Major*."

Ricard smiled. Desailles noticed and spared one second for a pointed glance at the heavily ticking clock on his desk.

"No, no longer, Major."

Desailles put down the pen he had been repetitively tapping against the gleaming surface of the desk. He flared his narrow nostrils and sucked in a quantity of the still air in the room.

"Well then."

Ricard lit a cigarette and placed it in the ashtray that Desailles had noisily slid towards him more out of some kind of courtesy than expectation that he would use it. As the smoke drifted up between them towards the small high window Ricard cleared his throat and began to explain what had happened.

...He had looked up in surprise when he heard Celine outside talking to the sentry, the man whom he had not expected to see again after sending him off to the infirmary on his very first morning here. Ricard had not expected to see her either, after her thin body had folded at the waist and crumpled, still folded, on to the mud-grey grass beside the tent. But the evidence of his ears was proved correct as the door opened. For a second her head was framed against the foggy light outside before taking on an orange tint as the light from the oil lamp caught up with her. She had smiled nervously and sat without thinking to ask on the opposite side of the desk. Her hands continually smoothed each other's skin, which went white under the covering of dirt. He had got to his feet uncomfortably at her entrance, but confronted by the thin lips and wide eyes he had sat down again, and then got up and strode heavily across the room to the door. He leaned outside to tell the sentry to get Sergeant Deloi to fetch some water, but also that he was not to be interrupted for any other reason. The sentry put a straight hand up to his helmeted head. Ricard closed the door and immediately felt the slowly moving air become still. A sense of nervousness shot up his legs and through his stomach. There was a tension in the soiled elegance of her posture. He could tell by her attitude that things were to be explained to him. He sat behind his desk again and took fresh paper and a pen. Then, belatedly, he greeted her.

"I am glad to see you on your feet. We do not have to discuss these matters now – you are weak, and I know it is painful to you."

She shook her head.

"I have to take my husband home. All soldiers want to go home after the war's over, don't they sir? My husband wanted to go home, even back to his job."

"What did he do?"

"He dealt with the accounts for some of the farmers near where we lived. It was boring – but he wanted, he wanted to go back to it."

"I have not gone home. Even I can see that here many men will not go home after this war. In the Caribbean, too, men are buried who will not go home. Why should your husband be different? I am sorry. I don't mean to be cruel."

He picked up the flimsy paper on which he had typed the latest draft of his letter to the family of Private Dessons. Sometimes the letters on the typewriter had pierced right through the paper. He could see fragments of her skin and hair through the gaps.

"When his family receive this letter his death will be worse for them than all the ones they heard about at Verdun. He should have been safe now, he should have gone home. But no-one wanted to try and save him, and now he's buried here. Why should your husband go home?"

She sighed and her hands shook slightly.

"Private Dessons should go home too, sir. When he died, he wanted to be buried in his own village near Nice. He had his family to go back to. If his body stays here I don't think his sister will ever have the chance to see his grave. But he's buried here now, sir."

"You know I cannot send him home without a warrant. It is in my orders to bury men here unless I am told otherwise by the Army. But come, please answer my questions. Why should your husband, in particular, go home? What has it to do with this place? I am sure it has something to do with Pericard. Something is clearly going on here."

The last few sentences of his speech jolted from his mouth. He had not meant them to come out, but they fell over his tongue like clumsy weights. He hated it when that happened. The place was obsessed with the dead, but his presence there was aimed at restoring some kind of life to it. The memorials on the battlefield had to be removed along with the other debris before any other men were consigned to the ever-growing graveyard.

She breathed in deeply and spoke. She told him that her husband had come to her two days after the telegram informing her of his death had come, how he had touched her forehead where she kneeled before the altar in their church. He had told her what he wanted her to do. She had agreed because she had wanted to give him something closer to his life than a grave in the cold east that was totally alien to him.

She came to Pericard as soon as she could after the Armistice knowing as little as he, the major, had known. What she sensed here had kept her long after most people would have given up hope. She could understand here what she had been unable to grasp even after her husband's death – that the war had been an act of robbery upon everyone connected with it – refugees, dead and bereaved.

A robbery made worse by the fact that no-one gained from it. Only the war itself could have profited and the scale of its theft had eventually brought about an end even to its own destructiveness – there had been nothing left to destroy.

"I know he will never touch me again but – don't you understand? I need him at home. He needs me to be near him. We are still in…"

Her speech faltered and she looked at him as though expecting some kind of interruption. He had not made any so far and he still did not speak. He had made a few notes on a piece of paper and the scratch of his pen had been audible over her quavering voice. She smiled, revealing stained teeth. Ricard felt his heart tremble slightly.

"It sounds unbelievable doesn't it sir?"

"Please go on."

Here was the place, she went on after a while, that those who had been most robbed, the dead, could reclaim some of what they had lost. And those that had been left with something to grasp on to, even if it was only bare life, could get restitution by helping them, by making the prayers that could no longer be made, by marking with their thoughts and their possessions the sacrifices of the dead, and by carrying out some of their wishes.

"That's why I must take my husband home. If I can, both of us will be able to accept his death more easily. There's no peace while the dead have their lives stolen from them."

"Stolen? But he died, as I have said, in the war. We won the war. France has been saved. If this was Germany I might be able to understand you. The dead in the war died to save France. As I said before, Private Dessons' death must be more painful to his family because it is peacetime, and the work he was doing was to erase the war, that robbed everyone… to give back to the people who were robbed because they lived here something of what they have lost."

"France may have won the war sir. The dead have lost their lives and I've lost my husband. The pain felt by Private Dessons' family can be no worse than my own."

Ricard looked at her. She had collected her scattered words now. She spoke quietly but with determination. She was strong enough not to be defeated by her own distress or his obtuseness. Another thought occurred to him.

"You say the dead wanted people to pray for them and presumably to remember them in the manner that I have seen, with the tokens on the battlefield – and the helmets and rifles. How far does this demand go? Am I doing wrong by seeking to clear up the places in which they died?"

She bowed her head. An expression of pain moved her lips and she closed her eyes. It was a long time before she spoke again. In the silence men's voices could be heard indistinctly. Ricard knew that they were engaged on the very work he feared that she opposed. At last she looked up again and let him meet her eyes.

"I know that one day the dead will be forgotten and the memorials will fall down. I don't know what will happen then. But for the moment – we – must give them as much peace as we can… sir."

"So did you *actually* discover whether there is any *real* opposition from the soldiers or the refugees, or people like this woman to our policy towards the fallen or to the battlefields themselves?"

Ricard stubbed out his cigarette. He was feeling slightly sweaty from telling this story to Desailles and telling it in such a way as to please the older man, as far as was possible. He pulled at his collar and looked up longingly at the tightly closed window. His chair creaked as he leaned back from the position he had unconsciously slipped into as he spoke.

"I do not know. She seemed to be confused about it. But I shall make further investigation. I shall speak to each of the officers individually. Incidentally, I have noticed that no-one ever talks about the German dead. It seems that only Frenchmen are admitted into this club. I do not know why sir. Though if you wish I can try to find out."

He added the last couple of sentences hurriedly in order to forestall the sarcastic criticism he could see forming on Desailles' lips. The major raised a quizzical eyebrow nonetheless.

"What was the answer to my question?"

"I have seen no evidence of it as yet."

This time it was Desailles' turn to lean forward. The light of the oil lamp shone off the bare patches on his head as he asked his next question.

"Well. Does *she* believe what she says?"

"I believe so."

"I might suggest that she is a little… *confused*. Might I not? She has been bereaved, she has lived in, as you say, *squalid* conditions and she has been frustrated in a desire that is close to her heart. It is possible that she is carrying some *physical* illness. I suppose you are aware that this flu epidemic has spread in the area. She *might* be fevered. Might she not be *convincing herself* of things that do not exist?"

"No!"

The force of his denial surprised Ricard. The source of it was a feeling that he had not yet confronted. Desailles looked at him with slight disapproval. Ricard blinked and swallowed and allowed his fingers to fall to the top of the desk and rattle slightly on the polished surface. He mentally cursed Blamanchard. He had begun examining his own behaviour in case it was like that of Desailles.

Now here he was, beginning to rattle his fingers. He cleared his throat and ordered his thoughts more carefully before he brought himself to continue.

"No, I don't think that it is only her who has lost her grip on things sir. If she has, then they all have. I…"

"*Including* Captain Deschaves?"

"He – I don't think so sir. I do have one concern regarding him, but he has provided me with important information as regards my theory."

"We will come to your *theory* in a moment. Captain Deschaves? What is this *concern* you have with him?"

"My views on Captain Deschaves should be considered in the light of what he has told me. Are you familiar with the story about Pericard sir?"

"I am. But… I think I would like to hear *your* version of it, or at least the version you have been told."

As the major completed his sentence he leaned back in his chair again. The pen in his long fingers recommenced its insistent tapping on the top of the desk as Ricard began speaking again.

In the uncomfortable silence that had followed the collapse of Madame Delain and her transferral to the medical hut Ricard had turned his steps towards the battlefield again in order to make an assessment with his own eyes about the clearing up. Without consciously thinking of it, he realised, he had had an urge to do something practical, impersonal, to escape from the issue of the death of a man under his command which seemed to him to be so utterly pointless. He also had to assuage a feeling at the back of his mind that he was neglecting his duties by becoming so bound up in the matters of "Additional". They were not his soldier's orders. His soldier's orders were out here in this mess of barbed wire, craters and bones.

He took the path made out towards the trenches that he had taken with Deschaves the day before. The ruts made by wooden wheels and by the feet of men and horses were filled with black water and pieces of metal. Around them lay heavy mud that weighed down his steps and splashed up onto the swinging edges of his greatcoat. He passed by the gun emplacement with a shudder as though he was running his hand through the collection of precious trinkets again.

For a long time he could see no-one. He was as alone as he had been when he had seen the simple memorials in the narrow trench. The stinking air closed round him as though he had put his head into the body of a turtle on the beach at Grenon. Then he spotted men bending their backs to shift something almost indistinguishable from the colourless grime all around them. Now he had seen them it was as though the whole area was crawling with the almost-blue figures, though in reality there were only three groups. He could see the figures of NCOs urging them on – or at least so it appeared. Their mouths were opening but the air was so lifeless that any sound they made did not carry even the short distance to him.

A little apart from all the groups he could see two officers – Vellard and Deschaves, he presumed, since Jannert had been put in charge of digging the graves for the dead men who had been found recently, a task he had accepted without enthusiasm, but also without protest. Ricard was gratified by the latter part of his response, but vaguely irritated by the former. It was easy to see, he was tempted to think, why the man had never risen above lieutenant. He made his way carefully to the two figures, fearing barbs, sharp metal or explosives.

As he drew closer he noticed that his initial reaction to the situation had been wrong. Deschaves and Vellard were not in conversation as he had supposed, but were simply

69

standing next to each other. Vellard's face was turned firmly away from the soldiers and from Ricard. In contrast Deschaves' head moved from group to group, scrutinising every movement that came within his field of vision. He noticed Ricard when he was still some distance away and saluted him. Vellard turned around reluctantly and his salute was so slow Ricard had looked away by the time it was completed.

"I thought I ought to have a look at what it was like to work out here after – what happened. I wanted to see properly with my own eyes."

Deschaves smiled and gestured grandly with his hand at the nearest group of men. One held the head of a draught horse. The hair of both was matted. Both heads hung towards the ground in an identical attitude of patience born out of endless waiting. Behind the horse stood a two-wheeled flat cart. At one corner of it the man's helmet hung at what seemed to be an impossible angle. The cart itself was piled high with debris – wire, spent shell cases, bits of rifles, pieces of sodden wood. Every so often one of the soldiers nearby would leave the thin line a little distance away with his hands full of something that was often so muddy as to be unidentifiable. Each handful was thrown with a clatter on to the cart. The men inched their way towards the uneven patch of mud on which the cart stood without a spark of eagerness visible in their movements.

"We will have to do this again, and again, and again."

Ricard turned around, surprised to hear Lieutenant Vellard's youthful voice. The man had a wry, rebellious smile on his face. He looked from Ricard to Deschaves as though assessing what impact his remarks had made on each of them. His eyes lingered longest on the captain.

"We will never clear it all away."

"It must be done, Lieutenant. Captain, please show me

what the other men are doing."

"As you wish, sir."

They left Vellard standing with the smile on his face. In his learned way Deschaves briefly outlined the problems that the men were facing. He showed Ricard the men dragging on the carcass of a gun and its carriage. He showed how other men were clipping slowly at an enormous length of barbed wire so that they could load it on to another cart. He showed him the three bodies they had found that day but had not moved because of the delay caused by the death of Private Dessons. A single sentry stood by the remains with his head uncovered and his rifle sloped firmly at attention. Deschaves spoke in whispers as he stood next to them. Ricard noticed that none of the bodies had helmets or rifles and his mind made an immediate connection with the memorial trench. He wondered if the Dessons' equipment had been the subject of a similar urge to mark his end.

He stepped away from the bodies in order to free himself from the feeling of being an interloper in the griefs of the sentry and the captain, which, though openly expressed, appeared to be too private for him to interfere with. Deschaves followed him, but kept his voice in an undertone.

"We are standing just a few yards from where Pericard used to be sir."

Ricard looked around him. The chaos seemed to be completely undifferentiated.

"How can you tell?"

Deschaves appeared to ignore the question. The tone of his voice changed, and Ricard felt that he was being lectured to again, as he had done on his first night in the village.

"The church stood there sir. There were stone houses running parallel to each other directly to your left. Near the church was the graveyard sir."

"You would almost believe that God had destroyed it."

Vellard had appeared beside him, apparently invisible in his movement.

"Lieutenant?"

Ricard began to wonder if the boy had even been sane before the war. Everything he said made sense on one level, but was total gibberish on another. Deschaves intervened with a sharp order to go back to supervising the work. Vellard snorted bitterly and stalked off to where the groups of men struggled. Deschaves turned back to his commanding officer.

"I am sorry sir. But be patient with him. He is young, and he did lose three brothers in the war."

"That's all right, Captain. You were telling me about the village. You said before that there was a story connected with this place."

Deschaves scratched his moustache and made an effort to laugh.

"I suppose I should tell you sir, given your orders. You have seen the consequences over there at the gun emplacement and in that communications trench. And this is perhaps the best place to tell it. Early in the war, before these trenches were dug properly and while there were still parts of the buildings visible above the ground, part of one of our regiments took shelter in the church here. Most got back to our lines, but one party was left behind after a sudden shift in the line. Such things were possible in those days. There were twelve of them. The remains of the church changed hands after heavy fighting a week or so later. Of the twelve men there was no sign except piles of spent rifle cartridges – like this…"

The captain bent down and plucked a corroded example out of a crust of earth.

"…a prayer book, and twelve marks of burning on what was left of the church's floor. Well – so the story goes, whenever this part of the line was in danger from an attack or a raiding party, these twelve men would return from wherever they had gone and aid the defence, somehow above the mortal defenders. When I first came here I met a man who swore that he saw a German fire at one of them only for the sniper to be killed by his own bullet… I don't know. It's an interesting story isn't it sir? Fantastic, I know, but it means a lot to the veterans."

Ricard tried to grunt a reply but his voice caught in his throat. In the ensuing quiet Deschaves let the rifle cartridge slip from his fingers and fall back into the mud.

"And what do *you* make of Captain Deschaves' telling of this story?"

"He tried to make light of it sir, tried to pretend that it was just one of those myths that soldiers invent. We had one or two about witch doctors, or voodoo or something on Grenon. But he told it as though it at least moved him. Whether he believes it, or half-believes it, I cannot say sir. He was right though. I think this myth is the key to understanding the high incidence of mental instability at Pericard."

"And Captain Deschaves?"

"He is a rather professorial character sir, which makes him rather distant…"

"He was a teacher before the war, in Nice I believe. Quite senior too, I am told. But that has little to do with what you were saying. Go on."

"He is not really part of it sir. I know he understands it all far more than I do, but he is not the same as Lieutenant Vellard sir. But that is where my concern about him is sir, concerning Lieutenant Vellard, I mean."

"In what way?"

"Well – he is very indulgent of the lieutenant's impertinence sir. It cannot be good for discipline, sir."

Desailles smirked to himself and then looked up from

the tightly written notes he had scribbled in the seconds when his pen could be spared from tapping. When he spoke the subject had been sharply changed.

"Do you know what *happened* to your predecessor?"

"Major Le Blanc? He went mad. Or became 'indisposed' as my orders so delicately put it."

"Captain Deschaves found him in one of the trenches *babbling* and smearing mud into his hair. A few days beforehand he had reported to Colonel Blamanchard that he was unable to feed all his soldiers any more because all the dead had *mutinied*. Interestingly he had been involved in *suppressing* the mutinies of 1917... I guess your theory now I *think*, Major Villier. *Hallucinations* of the dead? Brought on by *stress* and by the fact that there is a dubious *story* attached to Pericard. If this is the case, then you have given *two* examples – Lieutenant Vellard and... that officer's widow, whatever her name was. I have given one, Major Le Blanc. Any others? There *does* seem to be a widespread problem with morale here, and it also appears to have *medical* consequences that should not be ignored."

"Something along those lines sir. Incidentally sir the widow's name is Madame Delain."

He pronounced her name carefully, expecting Desailles to write it down. He did not, and Ricard felt a vague sense of exasperation. He briefly mentioned the soldier whom he had found in fits and the strange antipathy in the village towards bandaging the wounds of Private Dessons.

"Then sir, at the funeral of this private I have spoken of there were other minor suggestions that the atmosphere of the village revolves around the issues of the dead rather more than I had anticipated."

"I have heard an *estimate*, major, that nearly one and a half million of our men died over the past five years. It's *hardly* surprising that quite a lot of people are thinking about it. But I take your meaning in regard to *these* circumstances. Go on."

"Yes sir. Well – there were things I had expected. The helmet and the rifle presumably went out to the trenches, the coffin itself had a small silver chain placed on it during the night, but there were other things, I think. Perhaps it was just my imagination. Lieutenant Vellard did not attend the ceremony. As it was getting towards the end I heard shouts from the direction of the village. They lasted until the grave was filled and the last volleys fired over it.

"As soon as I could I went to investigate. I met the lieutenant on the edge of the village, and asked him what was going on. He wouldn't look me in the face, but eventually he muttered that it was nothing, that one of the villagers had had an accident. I realised that he wasn't being very helpful and so went to find the doctor, a Lieutenant Georges. He is a very scared-looking man. When I asked him, he looked blank for a few seconds, but I the end he supported what Vellard had said, adding that the man had been hit by a falling beam in the house he was building. I don't know, it is all very circumstantial, but it didn't sound very convincing to me. I spoke to Captain Deschaves about Vellard's absence, but he appeared not to pay much attention to me."

"That's when you began to have *concerns* about Deschaves' attitude towards the boy?"

"Yes sir."

Desailles dutifully noted all this down. Ricard licked his lips. He had rehearsed his long speech many times, to make it convincing to his audience. He knew that the group of events was unremarkable in itself, but to him they were the clinching evidence that some sort of mass delusion had overtaken the inhabitants of Pericard. Desailles had not seen the suspicion in Vellard's face or the hesitation in that of Georges. He was absolutely sure that the shouts had had something to do with the funeral of Private Dessons, and that, in turn, Vellard had had something to do with the shouts.

"Hm. I *suppose* such things might be significant. Have you managed to *trace* this villager?"

"There are three men in the village with injured legs. I am afraid I cannot say how they got them."

Desailles began to rattle his pen against his teeth. Ricard gazed at him without really thinking of anything other than a jumble of visual memories. At last he straightened his back and raised his eyebrows.

"I don't think I have anything more to report sir. Have you any new instructions for me?"

The rattle slowed to a steady tick-tock. After a few more seconds it stopped altogether.

"Keep an eye on Lieutenant Vellard with regards to *removing* him from duty – *carefully*, of course. Obviously, if you are worried about Captain Deschaves in this area, don't mention what you're doing to him. On a broader front, look out for any ways in which this whole myth of the dead thing can be *cleared up*, or *discredited*."

Then pen started clicking again, and Desailles looked back to his notes. Ricard supposed himself dismissed and slowly brought himself to attention. Feeling somewhat foolish, he saluted Desaille's bent head, all the time expecting the older man to glance up and ensure that military etiquette was being observed. Desailles did look up, but only as Ricard was opening the door to leave.

"Major Villier, *you* yourself are convinced that those myths are simply *myths*, aren't you?"

"Sir? Yes of course sir. I am not going to be drawn into any of that."

"I'm *sure* that Major Le Blanc believed that too."

Desailles smiled grimly before resuming his study of the notes. Ricard stole a last frightened glance at the lowered eyebrows and escaped into the corridor. For a few seconds he stood outside the closed door feeling a pain in his neck and eyes. The elation he had felt on his arrival in Rheims had now completely evaporated. He breathed out heavily, trying to relieve the strain, and turned towards the strange damp stillness of Colonel Blamanchard's office.

Jannert

He lay on his bunk, one arm beneath him, and tried to doze. But the noises haunted him, disturbing his rest from within, not from outside. Deschaves and Vellard had tried to reassure him, to help him accept all that had surrounded him, but even they had admitted that it would take some time, some days before the smell of rotting men stopped being so sharp in his nostrils.

He had been used to it before, of course. When his old school friends had been felled like corn and their bodies had built up in drifts like unholy snow around his home town, he had been used to it. But that had been a long time ago.

In the hospital where he had lain for months he had been able to smell putrefaction too, but there had been distractions, compensations. If he opened his eyes he knew that he would be able to remind himself of one of them. On the wall beside his father's crucifix hung the image of the nurse who, though married, had loved him enough to give him her photograph, which he had asked to be buried with him when he had believed his time was come. Her face still fascinated him, but here in Pericard the memory of the brush of her fingers had faded. She had slipped behind a noisy crowd. Each member of that crowd laid claim to him and he shuddered as the green-fleshed fingers clawed at him, pulled him different ways.

He had seen it in his men too. It was as though they were in a permanent attitude of flinching from the dead men's probing hands. Their shoulders were always hunched; their heads bowed lower than before. He

78

wondered if they, like him, found their disgust mingling with half-remembered pity. Like the sharp smell of rotting flesh, these feelings had once been familiar. He remembered cradling the head of a friend on the wet filth of a shell-blasted trench; he remembered the cries of the men at night wafting over no man's land as they pleaded to be shot. He had had to restrain himself as well as the men he commanded from climbing out there, gun in hand, to end their misery. Those nights when he had stood, his pipe in his mouth, not wanting to listen but unable to close his ears, came back to him with greater frequency than ever before. And the desire he felt to grant the dying men's last wish had grown stronger with each passing hour.

At last these reflections overwhelmed him. He did not pretend to understand, though Captain Deschaves and Lieutenant Vellard had pressed upon him eagerly the idea that he already did. They said he understood like the soldier whose visions, they'd said, he'd shared, and whose sentry post he had taken over from Major Villier on that first morning in the village. All that was needed, they said, was familiarity with the dead.

He sat up on the bunk and in the half-dark groped for his pipe and tobacco. It was a laborious business lighting the thing in gloom such as this, so he swung his legs off the bed and struggled to light the oil lamp on his trunk. The orange glow made him blink uncomfortably for a second but he gazed intently at his watch until he could see its face clearly. Major Villier was due to return this evening, in no more than a couple of hours. It would not be good for him to see his subordinates' faces looking pale and ghostly. A good pipe would help him look more presentable. He returned to the bed and prepared his tobacco. He could do this without looking too often at his fingers – another skill forced upon him by the trenches – so he spent much of his time gazing instead at the other photograph he had attached to his wall. This one was not framed like the one of the nurse. It was creased and folded in many places and often stained with coffee and other, less savoury, fluids. These were the marks acquired by a photograph that he had carried with him for much of his time in the trenches and which he had clutched at convulsively as they had stretchered his blood-soaked body from the battlefield. When the shrapnel had struck him his first thought had not been the pain – though that had soon occupied his mind – but the damage that the three-inch shard might have done to his photograph.

It was of his home town, Verdun. The city had been photographed from the air early in the war and the picture showed it in a transitional stage between the place he remembered as a boy and the shattered ruin he had left in 1916. The picture had been used in a briefing that he had attended and so there were lines on it and little labels that indicated defences and who occupied them. At the end of the meeting it had fallen to the floor near him and he had picked it up, rolled it up and stuffed it into a coat pocket before anyone had noticed. Since then he had spent long hours poring over it, tracing with his finger the streets around his father's house. He often walked there in his mind, on a sunny day when the grey buildings had taken on a sheen of colour and when familiar faces had seen and recognised him in almost every doorway. His legs remembered the pleasant sense of weariness that had overcome them when his round of deliveries and bill-settlings was done for the day and he was coming round that little corner with the butcher on one side and his father would be waiting for him with a cuff on the back of his head and the smell of food wafting down the stairs.

He idealised, of course. There were days when he had loathed everything there, and had wished upon it the fate that had now overtaken it. Those streets could now only be walked in memory and the faces he had seen were either dead, or thin and forcibly transferred to alien places. His father's was one of the latter sort.

The days when he had hated where he was were uppermost in his mind that last day with the old man. Everything about the place – its high walls, crowded streets and small-minded people always repeating themselves – had been evil to him then. He had resented the hard work and the poor money he had got in return. He told his father he was glad the shop had been destroyed since it meant that there was no reason, none at all, for him to go back to it. He had the Army now. When he had finished his convalescent leave he was going back to it. The old man, already frail since he had seen the devastation which had taken away his livelihood and, almost, his son, had broken down at this. He had tried to comfort him – it was his duty as a son to do that – but his father had wept still, and turned his back. He still found it painful to remember the shuddering aged shoulders in the ramshackle door of that temporary accommodation. It had been almost unbearable at the time, but with his friends gone and his home destroyed he had had to make a choice. His father had not agreed with him – so be it. He had been right to do what he did though. In the days that followed he had convinced himself of this. Verdun was finished by the war and there were few ties to take him back there. He had been right...

A plume of smoke began to rise gently from his pipe. The smell of tobacco penetrated and dispersed the rotting stench. The morbid thoughts that had oppressed him faded too. His shoulders relaxed and he turned away from the photograph. His neck felt stiff. He looked at his watch. There was enough time for him to take a walk and try and clear his head before Major Villier was due to return.

Celine

Celine realised two things soon after the accommodation for her and the other women was completed. The first was that the major had been paying her a great deal of not wholly unwanted attention since she collapsed on the day of Private Dessons' funeral. The second was that the strange ecstasy that had punctuated so much of her time in Pericard had not reappeared since the major's arrival. It had simply failed to occur. All that she received from her understanding now was a continual feeling of drudging anxiety with no end in sight, backed up by an undercurrent of grief, or loss. These sensations were consistent but without the occasional moment of exultation, brought about by another realisation that her faith in the dead was a positive universal, they began to seem unendurable.

She sat on a stool in the dim building as she reviewed her set of observations. She was hunched over, her body responding to the weight it could feel on her mind. For the first time in a long while she felt tired and dirty. She could feel the grime on her face, the sweat and the lice in her clothes. At the same time she could feel the well of resentment in the village reaching out to where the dead men still crouched in the trenches. Her eyes closed in weariness.

The slide into unpeaceful sleep was interrupted by a familiar firm knock on the door. She started to her feet, her brain struggling to cope with the opposing sensations of falling from the stool and standing up in alarm. She focussed her mind on the door. She could not sense any thought behind the rough pieces of wood. It was the major again.

"Come in."

He looked at her nervously as he had done every time he had come to visit her. The lines on his face moved slightly as he swallowed and smiled carefully at her. Celine bowed her head to him slightly and gestured, as she always did, towards a low chair that stood beneath the uneven table in the centre of the room. These meetings had quickly taken on their own rituals that they had both unconsciously fallen into. For Celine at least and, she guessed, for Major Villier, these regulated actions hid a great deal of embarrassment.

The major sat and carefully moved the clothes and pieces of rag with which the table was covered so that he could rest his arms on it. He turned slightly to the right and she knew he was surveying her thin form out of the corner of his eye because the light reflecting off it altered as she moved back towards her stool.

She sat down opposite him and wiped her lips with a wrist which was, she was suddenly aware, crusted with dirt. She was frightened by how much she noticed and was ashamed of these trivial physical details when the major was nearby. It was as though his lack of awareness of what went on in Pericard sent out ripples that affected even people like her. He was the cause of the mutiny of feeling in the village, that much was obvious, but she could not tell how much of this resentment stemmed from what he had done or from what it was thought he might do. She also began to wonder if that resentment had taken the place of the exhilaration she had lost.

"I am sorry I have not called on you for the last couple of days. I had to go to Rheims."

Celine waved a hand dismissively. She had only noticed his absence when the other women in the long hut had silently filed out at roughly the same time he had

83

chosen to arrive each day the previous week. They had left a sense of deference hanging in the air that she had felt guilty about. When it had become plain that the major was not coming they had come back in, trying to suppress the disappointment they felt. For them, she knew, she had become a voice that communicated with the alien presence in their midst. Beyond that there was a completely unconscious air of expectation that she could not fathom. Today that expectation had been far greater, for the major had only just returned when he made his way over to their house.

"Captain Deschaves says that you probably need more wood for your fire. I shall do my best to arrange it. I hope you are not too cold."

"Sir – we're not too cold. Besides it wouldn't matter even if we were. I've told you…"

"Yes, yes, Madame. You have told me. Your living needs will only matter again once your husband's body has been moved. You have told me. But though my errand to Rhiems was to report to my superiors, I had a second reason for going. I have handed your applications to Colonel Blamanchard personally and I have requested in the strongest possible terms that they be granted. I have done my best, and I beg you not to waste your time here if they are not granted, but I have done my best."

Celine's heart gave a great leap inside her. She felt the beat pulse simultaneously with the hearts of all the other women, who could not know the news, but felt her response. In her mind's eye she could see her husband start up from the filthy duckboards in the trenches and smile happily into the rain. It was only a vision because he would be with her when he heard, but it gave her great comfort. She felt another surge of affectionate gratitude towards the major.

"Thank you sir. It's a great relief to know that some

progress had been made. Major Le Blanc didn't do this for us, and he…"

"He said that the dead men of Pericard had mutinied. I really don't think he could have acted effectively in this way."

She reeled back, as though she'd been struck and the air had shot violently from her lungs. Her frustration at the wall of impenetrability around the major almost exploded. How could he offer this first practical sympathy and then undo the whole progress towards understanding he had made by offering this first direct denial of what she had told him? She had known that he did not understand, but now he was demonstrating that he did not want to understand! It was hard to grasp, but how could a fellow soldier be so deaf to the needs of his comrades? And she was so disappointed in him, such a good man…

"Madame? Are you all right? I'm afraid that living in those terrible tents has done awful things to your health, since you keep fainting. Here, take my arm... sit down. There. I will bring some you help... excuse me..."

His voice came to her through a cacophonic babble of protest. She could feel the future indignation of all those who had opposed her openness to him on the day of the funerals. Most prominent of all was the face of Lieutenant Vellard with its schoolboy top lip curled in contempt and its eyes turned with anger towards the invisible major. There could be no lies. They would know, and what they would do to him, and her husband's best hope of going home, she could not tell.

"In here... she looks like she's having a fit. God, she'll break her fingers!"

"Please leave us sir, I will take care of her."

The calm presence of Lieutenant Georges infiltrated her paralysed mind. As the door slammed behind the major she released her convulsive grip on the table top and moved her head to speak to him.

"I can guess what's happened. I've sent him away for a while."

"Thank you. I'm all right, I can stand up. They'll stop him! And my husband will never go home!"

Lieutenant Georges shrugged. He bustled around the other end of the hut trying to calm her worries by tidying some of the loose clothes that lay on the low beds. Celine watched him and began to wonder about the immediate violence of her reaction to what the major had said. She could not explain it except by the thought that she had believed him more understanding than he had just seemed. She was aware of her husband standing beside her again. Lieutenant Georges looked up and sent her an inward smile. He left the hut quietly, going to confirm the things others had felt.

"Hello Jean-Paul."

She stuttered out what had just happened. Her husband wiped her sweating brow with his rough fingers. He told her not to worry, he had faith in her, he knew that she had put a lot of faith into persuading Major Villier. He was sure the major would have the beginnings of understanding again. Then he added something about Captain Deschaves, that he thought he understood, but that soon he would be unable to. "His loss was so little – for him, no-one died." He looked apologetic as he spoke, as though repeating another's libel to offended ears. He kissed her many times, and then he left. Celine sat and tried to make sense of what he had said to her. After her husband's visit she felt justified in her flicker of affection for the major again, but there was also fear of the resentment he'd caused which had Lieutenant Vellard at its centre. It could only grow now, she knew. She must confront him – without Captain Deschaves nearby, all the more so because her husband had said those things about him.

As she straightened up from the washing tub she saw him coming in. He did not approach her, but went immediately to the – their – bedroom and left his things in there. He had not reached out to excite her arm with his teasing touch for almost three weeks now. She had not reached up to kiss his mouth for the same time, though she still washed and cooked for him. She did these things for him, though, like someone filling out a contract, or, closer, a jail term. A term which had lasted for many years and of which their were many years still to come. All this, and they had only been married three months, and he was going off to fight in another week.

A week!

She had not spoken more than was necessary to him since he had come home that evening with the letter. After a few days of near-silence he had tried to end the coldness with his fingers on her arm again, nervous, unsure where to go. But she had suppressed the faint tingling she felt at his attempt to restore what had been, and remained staring out of the window at the fields. He had lingered for a few more seconds like someone saying farewell to a loved place, then his arm had fallen to his side and he had tried to explain.

"I can't get out of it this time. It's the army or prison. They know about the last time and they won't let me get away with it again."

She had not answered. She believed it was possible for him not to have to go. He was just too afraid to try, She had never believed that he could be afraid, and that was why she was so angry. How could simple fear part them? They had been together for such a short time! Fear was no reason for them to be separated. The farmers had managed to protect him the last time he had been called up to serve. They had pleaded that he was vital for the produce of the area since only he could ensure that the farmers paid their taxes correctly. Now he said that this time their claims had been flatly contradicted by the office responsible. But the farmers liked him! He wasn't like the other scruffy youths who had been called up whilst sitting in a bar, looking as serious as they could, but passing round cigarettes under the table. No, he was more important than them, even though he had said the first time that the farmers had really protected him because of her, then a young sweetheart. She had blushed at this, and smiled, flattered. But she knew why it really was. It was him.

She had been waiting expectantly when he had come back that day, the last day he had really dared to touch her. The day before he had had nothing to do – some days there was no work, even for him. They had borrowed a cart from Le Mouri in the nearest house and driven the short distance to the coast in the hot sun. Her arm had been wrapped round him as he drove. As she remembered the wrinkles around his eyes as he squinted in the sunlight, laughing at something she had had said, her muscles remembered the shape of his back. The memory sent a pang through her and she looked down at the murky water swirling around his clothes in the tub, then up at his face which seemed thinner in light that seemed darker. She remembered how her face had felt severe and angry when she had looked up from reading the letter and how sharp her words had been. Their silence stretched between them.

A week!

She wandered down the wide space that served for the village's central street, trying to restrain the unreasoning panic that had infected her from the moment she had woken up. It had reached her through her dreams of Jean-Paul and the hot summer before the war. Anne had felt it before she had. She had woken before the others and sat nervously stitching damaged uniforms even before the

88

light had made its first gesture towards the little village. Celine had not spoken to her. She knew that the fear she was experiencing was infiltrating the minds of the women who waited for their dead men to come to them. It was eating into their sleep and soon they too would wake up to its full force and sit beside Anne, their needles moving to and from the thick cloth that they were attempting to repair. It would be in Lieutenant Jannert's face as he came to look at what they had done and offer his hesitant words of advice for improvements. She could feel no definite source of the fear except that it might be the first waves of the sea of resentment washing around their minds.

Celine's fear would not let her sit so patiently. She had gone out but could not quell it. She had to try and suppress it a little through contact with people who had not yet felt it. As she passed down the street the soldiers ended their morning parade and began to filter away from the ground near where the officers lived. She could feel the large cluster of their sensation splitting into smaller groups as they moved towards the duties that had been assigned to them. Two or three of these groups passed her. Some of the men bowed their heads to acknowledge her as she came near them. Others refused to look at her.

She was swept by starkly conflicting emotions – sadness, or anger. Occasionally the anger was so intense that it redoubled the force of her fear. The sadness did nothing to alleviate it, for it was a sadness of powerlessness, of men too used to being caught between hostility and incomprehension. She had almost reached the parade ground with its impotent tricolor roughly strung up on a flagpole when she felt someone urging her to stop. Sergeant Deloi and another soldier... Private Noilly.

"Good morning, Sergeant."

"Perhaps, Madame. Not for you, anyway."

"It's only fear. I'm used to that."

"I've been sent by Lieutenant Vellard, to bring you to him. But Major Villier has also ordered me to bring him Lieutenant Georges – they have to discuss the health of the soldiers, he says."

"I can't blame you. I know it's not easy, Sergeant."

"Private Noilly will escort you to Lieutenant Vellard. He has no qualms about it."

Deloi's weariness was suddenly overwhelmed in her thoughts by the intensity of feeling in his companion. It seemed that the private was no longer able to restrain his eagerness in going about the lieutenant's business. There was no respect for her as one who had come to Pericard by 'choice', such as she was used to. There was only the urgency of a man who desperately wanted to have things arranged as he wanted. Celine firmly addressed Sergeant Deloi.

"Thank you for coming to find me. I hope I haven't held up the major's business too long for your comfort."

Sergeant Deloi grinned, unexpectedly.

"I don't think so. Though we never know, of course."

"He seems forgiving."

"Yes."

There was a flutter in the feelings of both Sergeant Deloi and Private Noilly at the end of this exchange. Celine was unsure what it meant – anger, denial, assent... it was all of these but she could not tell from whom they came, though she supposed she could guess. Sergeant Deloi saluted her and went on his way. As his nervous thoughts faded she turned again to Private Noilly.

"Follow me, Madame Delain."

He led her through the rest of the village and out towards the battlefield. It was as though his feelings had been modelled on that vast expanse of chaos. They were, beneath a veneer of belief in Lieutenant Vellard, completely confused and ultimately undifferentiated – just a mess that he did not reflect on. There were no memories, such as were always present on the periphery of most minds, of life before the war. It was almost as though he had sprung fully-formed from the tortured earth, not the child of dragon's teeth but of spent shell cartridges.

He offered no sympathy or fellow-feeling towards her, only anger and frustration. Private Noilly thought the major was a barbarian... But then he had not had the benefit of the close meetings with him that Deloi and she had had. Sergeant Deloi, she realised, had emboldened her to defend the major in spite of what he had said the previous day. That little flicker in the sergeant's feelings during their conversation had told her something... that he had some kind of hope for the major... Celine had some kind of hope for the major. She had not lost it, even as she heard the voices of protest in her mind, and Jean-Paul and Sergeant Deloi had somehow kept it alive. This she must tell to Lieutenant Vellard. He was visible now. He was watching for them and reaching out to Private Noilly with a kind of aggressive affection that positively excluded her.

"Thank you, Private."

Private Noilly saluted, but before he turned away he fixed sunken black eyes on the young lieutenant. Celine felt a rush of imploring jolt out of his body, directed only at the officer. She only felt it because she was so close. Lieutenant Vellard acknowledged the emotion made exclusively for him with a short smile, and Private Noilly went on his way. Lieutenant Vellard turned to Celine and the strength of his resentment was like a stench that took away her will to breathe. Celine had forgotten what it was like to be confronted by something she found so repugnant. Yet the lieutenant's words did have some reason behind them. She could not deny that there was a case for him feeling as he did. He opened his mouth to speak.

"How long did it take you to cross France?"

91

"A – a month, I think?"

"It was not easy was it? And you came here for this, and knowing that you would have to stay with it for a long time."

Lieutenant Vellard indicated the battlefield with his arm. As ever, she could see it clearly. Even the scraps of cloth and used rifle cartridges were plainly visible. She shuddered, as she always did at the implacable grimness of it.

"Yes."

"I know why you came here, but tell me again why you stayed."

"You know why I stayed. For my husband."

"You were willing to sacrifice all for him. I will do the same for other soldiers. Here we can make good some of our losses, or at least give proper thanks, the dead want to be recognised, remembered."

"We can't get back all we have lost, Lieutenant. The major can see that."

Vellard spat. The motions of his mouth and throat seemed to be repeated a thousand times in the few moments while the phlegm was in the air.

"He only thinks in terms of dead men as dead, to put them in graves, to mark their names in some mass memorial."

"How do you know that?"

"He speaks like a man from Paris, or further away, I have seen the newspapers. They all speak of monuments and cemeteries. In Pericard we speak together, but we speak with our own voices, it makes a harmony under God like a choir. A cemetery, or a stone monument is only one note, only names, the dead are compressed by it…"

"I know, Lieutenant…"

"You know this, but you deny it, you side with him, you create divisions between us when you encourage this major to turn our Pericard into a Pericard for Parisian consumption, where people can marvel at the scale of it all and forget the men whose real graves they trample on in their eagerness to see the war!"

"Men from Paris died here too. I didn't encourage the major to do anything except help me get my husband home. He wanted to help me in that. There he sees a dead man's wishes and wants to fulfil them."

"One dead man – or a few, what kind of recognition is that? Here, by God's help we see the lives of many thousands each by each. For him there is one man, or a million names carved into anonymity on monuments."

"It's true for us too. You know it. My husband is close to me and I can see the men who died at Pericard. But what of all the others who did not die here?"

Celine's voice rose to match the boiling up of her emotions, but Lieutenant Vellard's assertions were more fervent.

"If Major Villier and his companions are allowed to see our dead in this way their lives are nothing…"

"Who can grasp a universe of dead men?"

"And so we must stop them, the battlefields must be left as they are so that in the ruins each man's death has its place. The dead men are saying, and God is saying with them – 'stop him', for he will ultimately destroy them and turn them into names, not men."

Lieutenant Vellard was in tears. The tide of resentment was now a tide of grief that drowned the sadness of the passive souls in Pericard. Through the lieutenant vibrated the direct sensation of all the loss felt by the village. Celine ran from him. What he felt was beyond anything her heart could withstand. She was amazed that he could survive all that feeling coursing through him. It was as though he had simultaneously died all the deaths and received all the telegrams bringing news of death of the last five years.

Was this his understanding? It was one so deep and thorough it could only blind him to all else. Celine ran, distantly aware of vomit in her throat through the increasing fear within her.

She found herself running frantically between the huts towards the major's building. Only there, she knew, would she be far enough from the shocks around Lieutenant Vellard's excess of comprehension. The building appeared in front of her suddenly, small and squat and running with water from the previous night's rain. Its iron and wood felt solid and firm beneath her hardened fingers as the ground never had recently. For a few seconds she leaned a hot cheek against it and rested her tired underfed body in the relative calm of the major's uncomprehending presence.

As she recovered her breath she began to hear voices inside. For a second she thought it might be Lieutenant Georges still, talking about 'the health of the soldiers'. But it was not. She knew by the light that her conversation with Lieutenant Vellard had taken longer than she had thought. This was different. A deeper voice, older. Sergeant Deloi! It seemed to that the major was asking him questions but that his answers were stuttering. Of course, he had felt the shock of Lieutenant Vellard's outburst too, even at a distance.

Celine moved herself along the outside of the building hoping to attract Deloi's attention through the wall and reassure him even though by now the waves of grief had faded and were becoming resentful again. It was difficult. Perhaps the major was between them. But she wanted to reassure the sergeant after the sympathy he had shown her earlier that morning. She had to catch sight of him at least. She moved towards the door guarded by the sentry. As she reached it the door swung open and Sergeant Deloi came out. He and the sentry exchanged worried looks. Celine ran up to them both.

"It was Lieutenant Vellard."

Then Deloi spoke, his voice tired.

"Major Villier thinks that the lieutenant is 'bad for morale'. I've been asked to summon him to be questioned."

"Don't! Not now – Lieutenant Vellard is in no state to see him. I'll go in. Find Captain Deschaves. Tell him to come here soon too. Perhaps he will have some solution."

As she spoke, Celine remembered her husband's enigmatic comments about the captain. But there was no-one else with enough authority to delay the major. Whatever happened, Lieutenant Vellard would not be controllable for a while now, and if he grew too angry – she did not want to see him suffer that pain again.

As she lay between the two blankets made of sandbag cloth that night, she wondered if Lieutenant Vellard might perhaps have been right. She had expected Major Villier's reaction to her appearance so soon after her last 'seizure' and she had struggled to convince him that she should be out of her bed. He had been overly concerned about her and she had asked him questions awkwardly, embarrassed, fumbling with words almost as her fingers fumbled with the pen he had given her to add her name to a document that made the applications for a permit formal.

"What are – how do they choose which permit to grant and which not to?"

The major had shook his head and smoothed his moustache thoughtfully.

"I don't really know. It might be something like the way they choose leave for soldiers – those who deserve it most. Perhaps if no other bodies will be brought home to your village…"

"What if there are many?"

"Who knows? I don't know why I was sent to the

Caribbean."

She had tried to question him about his war. Now she was in the room with him, away from the terrible spectacle of Lieutenant Vellard, smelling his cigarettes and the dampness of the wood and clothes, she wanted to prove the lieutenant wrong. Her husband would come home, and his first grave could fade away. Now she was here she could feel the sense of that again.

She had expected Major Villier's response to her. The conversation that followed was uncomfortable but not too alarming. She had not predicted Captain Deschaves. He entered almost without warning – the first she knew of it was that the major's eyes, now heavy-lidded from the water-filled air of eastern France, slipped away from her face and looked over her shoulder. She saw surprise replace concern, and then, only after that, she felt the captain's presence. The anger in it was only little compared to the multiple anguish she had sensed from Lieutenant Vellard, but it came upon her as a shock.

It seemed that Captain Deschaves was also surprised. He glanced at Celine with disappointed eyes but did not greet her. Instead he saluted Major Villier smartly. When he spoke his voice was louder than she ever remembered voices being, and there was a crispness in his movements that she had not seen since Major Villier had first come to Pericard. In the days that followed the major had gradually slipped into the quiet voices and gentle steps of everyone else, though never to the same extent. But now it seemed as though Captain Deschaves had freshly arrived from some overseas colony. As she looked up at his thin, scruffily uniformed figure she realised that what she could sense of his thoughts was rapidly disappearing, growing less distinct.

"I understand you sent for me sir."

"I did not. I sent Sergeant Deloi to find Lieutenant

Vellard and bring him to me. I have – matters I wish to discuss with him."

The major glanced carefully at Celine as he said this. There was a testiness on his voice that indicated exasperation. Celine caught the look and began to rise from her chair. But the broad hand of Captain Deschaves waved in her face signalling her to sit. She saw the dirt ingrained deep beneath long fingernails.

"I think Madame Delain should remain sir. It is she who last saw Lieutenant Vellard."

He spat the name out as though it tasted foul.

"...Very well. What do you have to say?"

"Sir, I propose that Lieutenant Vellard be relieved of his duty. He's a sick man."

Celine gasped. She put her hand to her mouth and looked down at the floor until the officers' gazes had left her.

"That is rather extreme, Captain. As you will know, I was going to interview him on the subject – but you have taken it upon yourself to pre-empt me."

"With good reason sir. Madame Delain, could you please outline to Major Villier the course of your most recent conversation with Lieutenant Vellard?"

"Were you a witness to this conversation, Captain?"

Celine shuddered, fearing his answer and not wanting to open her mouth. She felt sunk beneath the conversation which had reared up and over her, dragging her along with its own implacable logic.

"No, I was not, sir."

He shot her another glance as though expecting her to make some challenge, but she did not. She sat silent, waiting to be prompted again. He looked again down on her as she huddled on her seat. She waited. He cleared his throat and spoke again.

"I was a witness to what happened subsequently sir. I

saw from a distance that they had spoken together – you don't deny it?"

"No, no, sir, I don't. I did speak to Lieutenant Vellard a little while ago. He did seem – a little – upset…"

"What did you talk about?"

"About you, Major Villier."

"Really? In what way?"

"We were discussing the way you went about your – tasks, sir."

Her tongue limped to a stop. Its attempts to describe any of the significant parts of her conversation were hopelessly crippled because she simply could not describe them. Any language she might have used supposed an understanding that the major did not have, or could not have. He asked a few more questions, trying to establish what had been said, how upset the lieutenant seemed. She answered as best she could, but she could tell from what little she felt from Captain Deschaves that it was not enough. He was building himself up to a monstrous climax of fury and he wanted more support from her. She could not provide it. The sensations surrounding him were too alien for her to think of him as an ally. At last the major had finished his questions. She sat slumped when he turned away from her as though what he had asked had drained her of all the little health she had left.

"So, Captain, we have established that when Madame Delain spoke to Lieutenant Vellard he was not entirely himself, and he expressed, shall we say, doubts about my role here, and how I had been instructed to carry it out. Please now tell me what prompted you to demand that the lieutenant be removed from duty."

Celine bowed her head lower and willed him not to speak, knowing that he would. His voice was firm and sharp as though his words were being stencilled onto the air between the two officers. Major Villier still had not yet sat down but he reached absently for his cigarettes and matches as her listened.

"I found him in the trenches…"

"Just as you found Major Le Blanc? Or not?"

"In the trenches, yes, but not acting the same way. I didn't know you knew about that, sir."

"Why should I not? Go on."

"Yes, sir. As I said, I saw Lieutenant Vellard and Madame Delain separate on the edge of the battlefield proper. Lieutenant Vellard seemed very agitated, but he was heading towards his allotted post. I, of course, am supposed to oversee what goes on out there too, so I went to meet him."

"Where were you?"

"With the first team out there sir, as usual."

The major waved his cigarette to encourage the captain.

"I reached Lieutenant Vellard's party. He was – urging his men to empty the cart of the debris they had already collected, and scatter it back into the mud. He himself was treading what they threw on the ground into the earth – so that it looked as though it had always been there, I suppose."

"Were the men obeying?"

"Some, sir. Others were moving very reluctantly. There was not a lot they could do until I arrived. The lieutenant heard me shout, but he only looked up and carried on. The men stopped, but I had to restrain the lieutenant. And then – he was somewhat insubordinate, sir. If what he said hadn't been so mad-sounding, I would have demanded that you discipline him sir."

"The men were witness to this?"

Captain Deschaves blanched as though an unpleasant thought had just occurred to him. His voice was shaky when he spoke again.

"I am afraid so sir. There was nothing I could do to avoid it."

"I believe you. Well, where is he now?"

"I have put him into the care of Lieutenant Georges sir."

"I shall go and see him. You will accompany me?"

"I think, sir, that that would not be a good idea. I have had to have two men, volunteers, to restrain him."

"Very well. I shall go alone."

The major breathed a heavy sigh and put out his cigarette. His movements were weary, a violent contrast with the crispness of Captain Deschaves. He put on his long greatcoat which was becoming more and more flecked with the dirt of Pericard.

"Take your sentry sir."

Captain Deschaves' voice was urgent. Major Villier gave him a long tired look. Then he nodded. The captain saluted him, and followed his commander out into the grey rain. Celine sprang to her feet and ran after them, almost clinging to the tail of Captain Deschaves' coat as drops of water began to fall onto it.

Celine turned over in her bed. It seemed that she could not sleep even though the feelings of the village and the dead were at a low ebb. It was the memories of the day that kept her from her husband that night. She lay on her stomach and opened her eyes into the dark, and thought about Captain Deschaves. She had pursued him closely after the conversation in the major's hut until the major was out of sight. Then she had put out a quavering hand to grasp his shoulder and make him turn.

"Yes I know you're there."

He spat the words down at her upturned eyes.

"I saw what Lieutenant Vellard did to everyone – except me and Major Villier. Don't tell me I don't understand! I do. I fought, didn't I? He knows that! It's just revenge! Vindictiveness! Why am I excluded? What's happening? It's him! The bastard! How could he do this to me?"

All she could sense of him now was resentment and disappointment. And a lingering idea of Lieutenant Vellard. A confused idea… of affection and hate at war. She stammered. She had no clue how to deal with this strange aspect of his emotional tumult. No coherent reply came from her lips. A tension throughout the village between resentment and sadness silenced her as effectively as the fear of Captain Deschaves.

"He knows the answers! Has he locked me out of it? He said to me – what happened when the trenches reached Switzerland? What happened when the trenches met the sea? And I realised I didn't know! Did the Swiss have their own trenches where they sat and watched us kill each other? Were there trenches on the beaches? If so, then did the sea come in over them at high tide? Why did it never flow down to us? The worst is – if the trenches had to end somewhere – does that mean you could walk round them? Walk round the trenches! I don't understand. But he does, and you do. You have your husband, he has his God. God explains it all to him, and I realised that not once, not in four years did I call on God – my brother was safe, I was never wounded – I did not need God. But without God I don't understand- How could he do this?"

He coughed suddenly. She put out her hands again to steady his shaking frame.

"Lieutenant Vellard does not understand everything. I don't. I don't know what happened at Switzerland or the sea."

"But God knows – all these men prayed to God. The shrines – men were asking God – any god – to make sense of it."

"But He did not. He only made sense of the parts we needed to understand. Don't you remember? The war had its own sense. Jean-Paul told me that. It had its own sense."

Jean-Paul was by her now, whispering suggestions into her ear, supporting her with his cold arms and gripping her with those fingers that still had flesh on them. She could smell his breath so strongly. Yet Captain Deschaves could not see him. As he raged she could see his understanding slipping away. He was trying to make sense of it all and so everything that he knew about it all was leaving him.

Suddenly he fell silent. He stared at her angrily. At her ear Jean-Paul's whispering also stopped. She let her hands fall away from the captain's uniform. For a second Celine existed in complete isolation staring at the vacant figures, the decaying and the dead. She did not breathe. The captain seemed to be swaying as though in a strange breeze. Jean-Paul was visible from the corner of her eye, unmoving, watchful. Then the captain's face underwent a strange shift and emotion drained away from it.

"Leave me alone."

She watched him go, and slip on a stone that protruded from the mud. He swore but carried on walking. She turned back to Jean-Paul, but he had gone. Without even a suggestion of why. She swallowed the sharp pain of tears and eased back into the mass of emotion that swirled around the village.

Nothing had disrupted that mass for the rest of the day, while she had sat with the other women earning her food from the quartermaster by repairing those old uniforms. As she lay in the gloom she wondered if this was a good thing or not. Instead of the hundred or so moods she was used to, from the up-and-down hopes of children to the continuous moping of the village's older men, now there were only two. One bore the mark of Lieutenant Vellard. The other was so precisely in tune with her own feelings of bewilderment and sadness that she could not tell from whom it came. All the different sensations that were the essence of the village's understanding had been suppressed beneath this division. It did not lessen, as she had hoped, with the night. But still she watched and waited for a resolution that she dared not hope for. As it grew towards dawn she dozed fitfully half in and half out of a state of expectation that could not become anticipation.

She stared at him in the light that had begun to change, to take its colours from the fields outside. Slowly he realised that she was looking at him and turned his tired eyes up to meet hers. She crossed the room almost hesitantly, though within she was as determined now as she had been in the preceding weeks. She reached him, and, as though with sudden decision, ran her hand gently up his arm to his neck.

Light filtered through gaps in the fabric of the hut, and still she was awake, though most of the village was asleep. Strange images wandered through her mind, unformed and alien. Abstract shapes but still recognisable, a feeling that was like sound rushing through her body or rattling against her skull like the points of needles... Jean-Paul was there. Instead of the skull lightly coated with fragments of skin, broken lips and one eye gazing frantically left and right, instead of the crushed and lice-ridden uniform through which ribs and leg bones sometimes protruded, instead of the bloody saliva staining all down the body to the revolver belt and the gaping wound in the chest, instead of the stink of his own flesh and that of his comrades and of the rats and of the stagnant water out of which bones still showed there in the trenches, he was whole. His hair was carefully parted. His hands were brown and strong from the days in the summer of 1914. His eyes were kindly but afraid, just as they had been when he left that first time when the train had taken him off. As she sat up, she could see the gleam on the boots and the sharp folds in his new uniform trousers and the ungainly box in which he carried his personal belongings. He smiled at her and showed teeth, not shattered stumps. He put out his hand and touched her, and she could smell soap on his skin. And he was real. Not a dream, not the slightly distant figure she had grown used to. She felt the tears she had swallowed down earlier burst out of her, and her body began to shake with the seemingly limitless joy she thought she had lost for ever.

"Follow me."

She leapt into his embrace. He led her from the hut and out into the pre-dawn air, out towards the battlefield.

Ricard

So Lieutenant Jannert was injured. Ricard had been glad to hear that it was not too serious, since his other two duty officers were either ill or acting very oddly indeed. He had also been uncomfortable for the last few days as a result of the disappearance of Madame Delain, an event that had troubled him more than it should. His thoughts had often been directed towards her from the very first time he had met her. Now she was mysteriously gone he found himself dwelling on her more and more. This was not like him. It would be too great an irony he reminded himself if he, who had rejected familial attachment, should be drawn to her. In any case he could not forget her husband and if *he* could not…

He had sent men out to search for her, but when they had returned empty-handed he had still had peculiar dreams that featured her and a heavy coffin. Perhaps the most positive thing about the injury to the lieutenant was that it would allow him escape his continual grappling with the odd events that had surrounded Pericard and to get to know the reclusive officer. Lieutenant Jannert had barely spoken, it seemed, since Ricard had encountered him that first morning after a 'bad dream'. He reached the medical hut and was greeted by Lieutenant Georges and his reassuring smile.

"How is he?"

"He's fine sir. These injuries do happen a lot when people are carrying out this kind of duty. He'll be back on his feet in a few days."

"How did it happen again?"

"He was helping the men shift an old gun carriage when he slipped and it glanced off his leg on the way down. Just a bit of bruising really, but it makes it hard to walk sir."

Ricard grinned at the doctor. It seemed to be impossible to be tense about the situation since even the medical man was treating it lightly. That impression was reinforced when he was led to Lieutenant Jannert's infirmary bed and found him flipping idly through the pages of Captain Deschaves' copy of *Les Miserables*. On the bed beside him were a few pieces of cloth – it looked like old uniform material – stitched together in a variety of ways. Ricard found himself staring absently at them. He pulled his thoughts back to the situation just as Georges, with a grand sweep of his hand, indicated the patient.

"Here he is sir."

"Thank you."

Lieutenant Georges bustled away to his office.

"Good afternoon sir."

"Good afternoon, Lieutenant. I was wondering how you were."

Jannert's hand wavered in the direction of his pieces of cloth, but he did not go so far as to pick them up or conceal them. He asked his superior about the work in the trenches and they spent a few minutes discussing it. Jannert made a few suggestions about it and Ricard tried to remember them. But the lieutenant's mind wasn't on that – his interest seemed desultory and begrudged. There was something else hovering behind his lips. He looked at Ricard imploringly, or so it appeared. Ricard was pleased. He could read the man easily and he could give him what he wanted. After all, to talk was why he had come.

"Are you happy here? Sorry, maybe the word 'happy' isn't the right one to use. Are you…"

"'Happy' will do sir. Compared to what went on

before. Though I am looking forward to the future too, even if what I'm looking forward to might be a bit peculiar."

Ricard saw that Jannert was looking narrowly at him, apparently expecting some encouragement. He deliberately took the bait.

"Really?"

Jannert smiled nervously.

"I've been thinking about it a lot since I ended up in here, and it seems like a good idea."

"It probably is, if you've been thinking about it."

"I'm going to apologise to my father."

"Your father? The tailor? Why should you apologise to him?"

Jannert breathed in deeply. When he spoke he seemed to do so like a man trying and eager to work something out in his head, though the words came quickly enough.

"My father worked very hard and was not successful. It's something of a family trait. After the war I decided I would throw in my lot with the army – I didn't want to work as hard as he had for so little reward. My choice upset him. His hard work wasn't even being recognised. And recently I've realised that he had a right to be disappointed – I thought I could do better in the army, but all I am is a lieutenant. Did you know, sir, that I advise the women on the repairs to the uniforms?"

"No, no I didn't…"

"I've been practising again. As with these."

He waved the pieces of cloth apologetically under Ricard's nose. Ricard frowned at them. They didn't look like practice to him. They looked like pieces of evidence in Jannert's rambling case.

"If I'm going to fail I may as well do it properly. That's another family trait you know, doing things properly. That's why I haven't gone already. I have to

107

finish my term, do the job to the end. But I *will* leave the army at the end of the year, and go home to do my job, and see what they have done with my home town."

"I'm sure it won't be as good a job as the one we do here."

Ricard winced at his own lame heartiness but Jannert did not appear to notice.

"Maybe sir. It does feel better to be doing for the people here what people are doing for me at home. It'll be strange when I get there. But when I do I will have lived through it all and found my life again. My father will be a happier man, and... I don't know if you'll understand it sir..."

He paused and cleared his throat.

"When we were fighting there were some local ones amongst us who just hoped that enough of us would be able to go back to carry on our families and our jobs and everything like that. I'll be going home for everyone who won't, or who are buried there and whose home was outside the city. Do you know what I mean sir?"

It felt as though the second reason was more important, since the lieutenant's words became forceful and he looked downcast when he spoke of the Verdun men who had died. Even so, through most of his words there was an optimism that Ricard did not remember seeing in the gaunt uniform-frame who had accompanied him to the village. Jannert, having waited for a response, started again.

"I finally understood when I got here sir, when I realised that this place has an importance like everywhere else on the front line. Everyone here wants to go home, or be thought well of, or remembered sir."

Ricard sat silent for a few seconds when Jannert had finished. He looked into the other man's eyes and thought he saw a desire for approval, as if his subordinate was unsure of what he had just said and was requesting some sign that he was not completely wrong. Everything he had said had been offered up for examination. Ricard chose his words carefully.

"I don't think I've ever heard you say so much. It's quite pleasant to find someone who has control over the way his life will go."

This did not seem to be enough. Jannert still looked at him. He picked up one of the pieces of cloth and surveyed the neat stitching.

"I'm sure you will do well, better than you expect, when you go back. If you are only practising here..."

Jannert's expression was rueful. His voice had an edge of disappointment in it. Ricard felt mildly embarrassed at having failed some sort of test. He wondered if there was something else that the lieutenant was trying to communicate, something that he did not understand at all.

"You mean, if I'm only practising what will happen when I start to do the job properly? Thank you sir."

There was a brief pause. Ricard decided to build on his success at making the lieutenant talk.

"I suppose you've heard of Lieutenant Vellard's... indisposition."

"I have, sir. A sad business."

"I'm afraid that he's deluded. He has wild hallucinations about the war. It's only to be expected in some men, I suppose."

"Indeed, sir."

"Such delusions seem very common here. Have you had any experience of them before, during the war for example?"

"Not like – what Lieutenant Vellard sees, sir."

Ricard looked down at his subordinate. It looked as if he had been right in thinking that he had failed to understand something in the previous conversation. Where the enthusiasm had been now there was only a closed face.

He thought he could see a pale hand fidgeting towards the pieces of cloth, and a twitch in the leg that was tightly bound with supporting bandages. Ricard's mind twinged with annoyance, both at his own lumbering questions and with the inscrutable motives of a man who even in the last war could not rise above lieutenant. The two together had defeated him. But he still wanted to know this man. He tried his last tactic.

"You may be aware that Captain Deschaves and I tend to meet at my quarters early on Wednesday evenings to discuss the progress – or otherwise – of our work. It's an informal meeting, but very useful. I am sure, from our conversation, that you could contribute. When you are well, feel free to join us."

"Thank you sir. I might."

"I'm sure you will, Lieutenant. Now, I am afraid I have things to do. I am glad to see that you are recovering well. I shall see you up and about soon, no doubt."

"Thank you, sir."

Ricard walked quickly out of the faintly chemical smell of the infirmary with a smile twitching on and off his face. It was not a smile of particular joy, but one of a man who had successfully gained his objective. Without actually giving any orders he felt sure that the frustrated tailor had been left with very little choice about whether to attend his meeting or not. And the more he spoke to the man the more he could rely on him.

In the open air, he forgot about his failure to grasp what Jannert had been trying to communicate. The rhythmic squelching of his feet in the mud, and the generalised hum of village and military life seemed to turn his mind in on itself where it began to compare what Jannert had told him and the half-crazed and crazed stories of Madame Delain and Vellard.

Without really thinking about it, he had arrived at his

own quarters. The ragged hair and folded face of the sentry suddenly jolted onto his consciousness and the question, asking if there had been any messages for him, burst from his mouth. He had got into the habit of asking every time he came back in case there had been any news about Madame Delain, or if Lieutenant Vellard had done anything. When the sentry shook his drooping head and shrugged shoulders clad in a patchwork of repaired uniform – a fleeting thought of Jannert – a sense of disappointment ran through him and he was no longer able to concentrate on the issues that had occupied him for the last few minutes. Instead, the smell of damp around the man, the rough feel of his door which always promised splinters, and mud falling from the soles of his boots as he knocked them against the door post occupied his mind until he was inside.

There he moved around erratically, taking his coat off and pouring some water for himself from a jug. For a few seconds he stared at the place on the wall where Major Le Blanc's crucifix had hung. Then he moved over to his desk and stared at the photograph of the anonymous woman in her elaborate frame. His mind gingerly probed at the problem of Madame Delain as he scraped a fingernail up and down the gilt carvings in the photograph's frame. All at once he pulled himself together, drank out of his metal-tasting mug and flipped through the papers on his desk.

From the pile he selected his second, and latest, report for Major Desailles, which he was supposed to be rewriting. He turned over the introductory pages and began to read where the main body of the report began, with his encounter with Lieutenant Vellard after Deschaves' peculiar visit to his quarters. He pursed his lips as he scanned the untidy typescript for the right point. As he found it, he pulled his cigarettes from his tunic pocket and forced his paling forehead into wrinkles of concentration again.

"I proceeded at this juncture to continue the investigation myself, and left my quarters in order to intercept the soldiers whom Captain Deschaves had informed me were bringing the lieutenant into custody. I encountered them approaching my quarters at great speed and without Lieutenant Vellard. Both were in a state of agitation, and reported that the lieutenant had escaped their custody and returned to the battlefield. One of them appeared to be satisfied by this turn of events. I chastised him and instructed him to remain with me while the other went to fetch his company sergeant and at least four other men in order to fully secure the escaped officer. This detail soon arrived and we progressed on to the battlefield proper. Men were sent to each of the details engaged in clearance work in order to gain any reports of sightings of Lieutenant Vellard. The remainder of the party I instructed to move more carefully towards the 'shrines' in and around the trenches where I suspected fugitive to be. As I have indicated before, it is generally thought that Lieutenant Vellard feels a great deal of affinity with these examples of memorials to the dead.

"In the event, my hypothesis proved correct. Lieutenant Vellard was identified by one of the party having concealed himself in the remains of a trench. One or two of the party seemed reluctant to apprehend him but they did not overly impair the success of the attempts. I instructed that Lieutenant Vellard should be brought under restraint to a secure place in which I would inquire in to his motives for acting in such a way as he did. I left instructions that two men be left outside the door of the chamber in case he grew violent.

"I will attempt to record the subsequent conversation verbatim so far as I can, as it sheds some light on the situation in the village with which you and I have been concerned:"

Ricard frowned and paused and crossed out some of the more formal phrases with heavy pencil lines. This dry report was completely alien to the sweaty, stagnant smelling chase between ruined equipment and collapsing mud walls. The pursuers had slithered and fallen on their knees in the thick mud. They had become splattered up to their necks in the macabre chase through the silent detritus, and added new marks to the churned ground. Ricard's own thin shouts had sounded feeble in the heavy air, but the whoops and laughter of the fleeing lieutenant had filled space easily so that everything around the desperately running men had seemed to be mocking them, as though the war was enjoying another grim joke like the death of Private Dessons.

The bizarre game had continued while men's legs grew tired and the mud seemed to be tripping them maliciously. Vellard's form was ever more indistinct as though he was disappearing into the battlefield, and luring them after him. Ricard felt his arms flailing left and right in increasingly incoherent signals. His self-control foundered as the men scattered, regathered and scattered again and Vellard stayed out of reach of their weakening hands. The chase was an eternity and Ricard felt that he had spent so long amongst the debris that his eyes had forgotten that there could be colours.

Eventually it was he himself who broke the complicity between the battlefield and the lieutenant and became Vellard's inadvertent captor. He had been standing shouting while his men had run this way and that, when a sharp blow in the back had sent him sprawling, pushing his face into the shiny filth and grinding it between his teeth. He still shuddered as he remembered the taste and the colour of it when he had spat it into his basin that night. Lieutenant Vellard had slipped as he had tried to avoid his commander, and in falling had brought the chasing to an end. The more enthusiastic men had pressed him into the mud and knelt by him, panting and filthy while Ricard had given them their next orders.

"'Lieutenant Vellard'," I stated, 'you have been apprehended both for your own safety and for the morale of the soldiers in this area. Can you offer any explanation for your behaviour?'

"'It's you! You will betray us all!'

"Lieutenant Vellard behaved very aggressively toward me throughout this interview, but did not offer any physical violence. I attempted to be patient and understanding throughout, but this had no discernible effect on the attitude with which he conducted himself.

"What do you mean? Please explain in what way I, an officer of the Republic, am betraying the citizens of that Republic?"

"'See? That only goes to show how little you understand – they died for the Republic! They lived in shit, and you want obscure them so we can remember the Republic and not the men who died for it. So you can say "this battle killed this many, that battle that many" and not know who the many are. Even Deschaves sees more than you!'

"'Captain Deschaves? Why do you mention him?'

"Vellard grinned rather disconcertingly at this point. I let him make his enigmatic answer – which I will take up and investigate at the first opportunity – and changed the subject. The answer he gave was: 'I could hardly not mention him.'

"'You are suggesting, then, that I wish to eradicate the memories of the dead? I am not doing that – I am merely returning the other victims of war to their rightful homes.'

"'And cover over the marks of the battles so you no longer have to smell them! And build neat cemeteries and artistic memorials so you can forget the dead as men and how they died! They did not die for you, or for Paris, the men who died were men of families and lovers and teachers and farmers, they died for those versions of the Republic. All different, like the men, with different wishes and dreams and hopes and you want to build a memorial of the War over them, not monuments to them themselves! The only monument to them that can be what is out there – in the 'shrines', the helmets and rifles, the little messages they wrote themselves saying what they wanted – to go home, to see their wives – anything!'

"At this point Lieutenant Vellard broke down in tears. I continued to question him gently.

"'How do you know this? Don't you think that the grief expressed by the nation as a body towards the men as a body might not be enough? Surely we must move on, and carry on with life. The war was terrible, but it must pass.'

"'It must pass? Pass? How can it pass for all those men except to see themselves forgotten, their wives marry again, their children adopt new fathers? All their wishes and desires must shrivel and be neatly swept up by you along with their bodies. Listen! Can you not hear them protesting against you?'

"It did seem as though he was actually listening for a noise that was real to him. Lieutenant Vellard is a young man and it seems that his experiences during the war have badly upset his mind. He does have a small following amongst the soldiers and villagers, but most are suspicious of him as far as I can see. You will note the interesting parallels however between his ravings and the comments reported by me to you of Madame Delain about her husband..."

There followed some inconclusive musings. Ricard crossed them out sharply. So sharply that the paper tore under his pencil. He scribbled in some comments about the parallels that were now crystal clear to him between what Jannert had said to him and the other two examples.

"Each of these three people derive consolation from the idea that they are acting for the dead – Madame Delain for her husband, Lieutenant Jannert, apart from his father, for friends and neighbours, and Lieutenant Vellard for the war dead generally. Perhaps this is a common result of the trauma engendered by the war. I would be interested if you could find parallel examples in other areas and how widespread these are. The only fundamental flaw in my theory that these delusions and hopes are developed as a self-defence mechanism is that Lieutenant Vellard seems to be as traumatised by his consolation as much as by the war itself, and that, in addition, he seeks to traumatise others. However, as I have observed above, he is a young man; perhaps his mind is insufficiently practised in dealing with suffering generally, not just that caused by the war. His response to his perceived communication with the dead then is perhaps the extreme one of an impressionable youth."

It was perhaps slightly self-contradictory as a report. Ricard shrugged. He could not be bothered with the niceties of editing at this point in time. He stubbed out his second cigarette, which had been burning down unnoticed in the ashtray by his elbow as he typed and pulled the paper from between the heavy rollers of the typewriter with an effort.

For a few seconds he gazed at the sheet of paper, his eyes picking out phrases here and there which he surveyed idly. From scribbling suggestions to himself he had gone to writing formally and then to typing rapidly, always impatient to be getting on with the next stage. He had one more section to complete that evening, and it was the nagging presence of it that had kept him at his desk until his neck ached and it felt painful to move his eyes in his head. Perhaps unconsciously he had been hoping to put it off until tomorrow in a sort of expectation that it might be resolved one way or the other.

He forced his attention to turn to what he had just written. He knew that he was going over a lot of the ground he had already covered in his interview with Major Desailles, but it did no harm to have it set down in writing, particularly since he had written what he thought he would have been hard pushed to put into coherent speech. But now there was this last matter, this last paragraph that he was afraid of because he did not want to be seen to be worrying too much about a non-military matter, nor to be seen to be not taking care of the people over whom he was in actual, if not nominal, control. Nonetheless he had to write it, even if only as a means of purging his feelings about it. To have his concerns about Madame Delain down on paper was important. Perhaps he could trap them there so that at night he would no longer be disturbed by long hours of worrying and feeling that she had gone for good.

He stared at the typewriter in the lamplight and realised that the orange was breaking its proper boundaries and was swirling in the air. Sometimes, on the corner of his vision, it seemed to form or outline figures that watched him as he sat. He knew they were optical illusions brought on by sitting and staring for too long in artificial light, and he did not even bother to move his eyes towards them to make them spill into blobs of light. Nonetheless, their presence did bring to his attention his need to get outside where it was cool and where he could stretch the itchy twitchiness out of his calf muscles.

In Pericard it was dark and only candles gleamed here and there throughout the gloomy shapes of the village. Gazing at them Ricard was unable to suppress a yawn and a lingering thought of his bed. Still, it was pleasant to feel the cool breeze. Ricard stretched his arms and felt his muscles begin to return to their usual shape. He nodded amiably to the sentry, who saluted back, and began to walk slowly, playing in his mind with phrases with which he could begin his account of the disappearance of Madame Delain.

Without really realising where his footsteps had taken him, he found himself on the edge of the battlefield where the breeze blowing from the village could only add to the stink of the turtles a slight tinge of woodsmoke and the strange smell Ricard recognised from his boyhood as that of cold winter air and wet ground.

He turned his back on the wrecked land and looked towards the first attempts at its reclamation in the shape of the village. He could barely see it, but its presence was reassuring. At his back he could feel the old village and its mysterious church, and with it, the immensity of the empty space that stretched to his left and to his right from the border of Switzerland to the coast of Belgium. He could feel that in all those hundreds of miles there was nothing but rats, some straggly grass, and corpses, dead men still guarding sentry posts, staffing bunkers and even fighting battles. He shuddered and reminded himself that he was tired and that he had done nothing but think about those men and their companions all day. He was not reassured by the possibility that Madame Delain was lying out there injured.

That thought could only darken his mood. The feeling that he had his back to a gargantuan cavern out of which something might reach and take hold of him remained. He turned round slightly to reassure himself. Only yawning gloom greeted him. This only heightened his sense of being a small isolated speck on the crumbling edge of an infinite space. He moved his shoulder blades tensely as though expecting a blow between them. Despite the pleasure that the coldness of the night had given him, he decided that he had lingered too long outside. With his back still turned towards the vacant expanse of the battlefield he walked quickly back into the circle of the village where candlelight seemed to warm the cold sweat on his body.

"Any messages for me?"

"Yes sir."

"Well? Spit it out man!"

"Sir – Sergeant Deloi inquired if you were wanting to eat sir. I said you'd gone out, he said he'd come back."

"I see. Well – if he does come back, please tell him that yes, I would like to eat, but that I am not to be disturbed otherwise…"

"Yes, sir."

Ricard stamped irritably into his hut. The news of a message had cheered him up immensely, and to find that it was only food and not a solution or a lead in the Madame Delain question was very annoying. He was hungry though – and cold. He suddenly noticed his greatcoat hung on the back of his chair. He shrugged it onto himself muttering angrily – how could he have forgotten it and not noticed until he was back inside? He made a mental note to ask Sergeant Deloi for some coffee when he arrived.

He began to wonder if he should really have decided to devote the day to writing reports. It could have been split over two days, after all. But then he had already arranged for Major Desailles to receive them the next morning. It had to be done. As soon as he had warmed himself up he hung his greatcoat behind him again, and covered the typewriter with its dust sheet. It would not be needed yet because he expected to have to do two or three drafts of what he was about to write. For a few moments he stared into space. Deloi's voice outside disturbed him for a moment and he almost grunted at the thought of being interrupted. But he sighed instead and began to write laboriously, with many crossings out.

"On the morning of Wednesday last, it was discovered that Madame Delain, of whom I have written and spoken to you before, was no longer in her quarters. I was not alerted at first because such a situation, while far from the norm, was not seen as being sufficiently peculiar as to arouse suspicion. She was not seen for the whole of that day, and when she still had not put in an appearance the following morning, one of the women, Anne Lamarque, who also has an application for a permit (to move the body of her son) pending, informed Sergeant Deloi, who in his turn, brought the old woman to me. As a result of my questioning of her and of the other women who share that particular set of quarters, I established, so far as I could, the facts of the matter, namely:

"Madame Delain had given no indication of her impending departure; she had not taken any belongings with her – including passport and papers; she had been very upset that day – it was the day of Lieutenant Vellard's arrest, as you may recall. Further to these inquiries I enquired of Captain Deschaves if he had seen her. His answers were contradictory, but as it transpired he had spoken to her that day and she had parted from him in extreme agitation. Other witnesses corroborated what I was told.

"As you are aware, I am of the opinion that Madame Delain is not a little confused by the series of events that began with her husband's death. I have related to you the peculiar nature of her beliefs on that subject. I contend that..."

At this point Deloi entered with a heavy tray of food. Ricard looked up from the paper with a guilty start as though he had been caught writing libels about Clemenceau. He instructed the man to put the food on the low side table, and to bring some coffee in an hour, and not to disturb him otherwise. Deloi fled as quickly as his dignity would allow him. Ricard looked down at what he had written and was exasperated to find his concentration broken. He had done well, he thought, as he had done with the account of the capture of Vellard, to keep his emotions quietly wrapped up away from his pen.

Here, for example, he demonstrated as to an invisible Major Desailles, there was no mention of the infectious panic of Madame Lamarque... no hint of Captain Deschaves' hesitation which had led to Ricard's first serious fury in the village and the captain's instantaneous capitulation. He had been doing well. And now, he had to write an account of the following days without the persistent, nagging anxiousness seeping from his hand and sleepless head to the pen and diluting the functional ink.

"...the alarming experiences of that day unsettled the already unstable condition of her mind, and she has left the village under the influence of that unsettling. In the light of her recent medical record I am unable to conclude what will be the final consequences of this event. She has twice succumbed to fits and twice recovered surprisingly quickly. The chain of events suggests that this indisposition is temporary, and that, if in the course of it she has not injured herself sufficiently as to be rendered immobile, she will return. On the other hand, the two fits have proved just how great a cause for concern her mental state is.

"Her apparently rapid recovery in both cases may well be a sign of increasing bodily weakness rather than strength. This third fit may well prove to be permanent. I do not claim to be medically competent to judge the probability of either result being the correct one. I have discussed this with Lieutenant Georges, but he claims to be similarly unqualified in this area.

"Though this is technically a non-military matter, I am sure you are aware of the importance of Madame Delain to my research into the state of mind of the soldiers in Pericard. I have sent out search parties in all directions in a circle of some miles in diameter, except for the battlefield which is being quartered by extra details as well as the men who are working there normally. So far no trace of her has been found.

"May I request that in addition to these ongoing searches, that any woman without papers who matches her description (appended) be interned by local authorities and questioned in case it is her. I must also request that her application for a permit to move her husband's body should not be suspended or delayed. If she does return any indication that such a course has been taken could have far from positive consequences. As I have stated, the searches continue, but optimism amongst the searchers is rapidly declining…"

Ricard stopped. By his watch he only had a few minutes before Sergeant Deloi was due to bring his coffee, and he had still barely touched his food, only occasionally seizing on a lump of bread or a few stunted vegetables as he walked around the room trying to construct a firm edifice of statement around the emotive facts. But now his hunger had taken a firm hold of him and he had to eat. He shovelled the cold food into his mouth, ignoring the taste and concentrating on the feeling of packing out his stomach walls. After a short time he had eaten almost all of it, and he poured water on to the mass inside him to soften it and relieve the slightly uncomfortable tightness it caused. When Deloi entered bearing strong-smelling coffee, he was seated behind his desk again, attempting to order the papers on it into sensible ranks so that he could find what he wanted.

"Your coffee, sir."

"Thank you."

"Anything else sir?"

"No, not really. Oh – just one question – for the purposes of my reports, you know. Do you believe that we will be able to find Madame Delain?"

"I don't know sir."

"A straight answer please, Sergeant."

"If you want me to answer honestly, sir…"

"I do, Sergeant."

"In that case, sir, I don't think so, sir."

"Very well, Sergeant, thank you. You are dismissed. Duties as usual tomorrow."

"Thank you sir."

The door closed behind him and Ricard stared at his paper in the still, oil-fumed air. His report was factually correct, then, not just an assumption made to express his own feelings on the subject. It was odd, he thought, that he had been able to pass a judgement on someone's chances of survival with such economy as this: "optimism amongst the searchers is rapidly declining". His own anxieties and the slight, sad jerk of Deloi's head as he had given his opinion were completely suppressed under the factual clarity.

This was entirely a good thing. He could not have Major Desailles believing that he was going the way of Major Le Blanc. And anyway, what would be the point of

123

going into detail over it? His head dropped and his shoulders slumped. He felt very miserable. But what had to be done had to be done. He admitted that the disappearance of Madame Delain was on his mind more than it strictly should have been, but there was no need to make the situation worse by delving into the whys and wherefores. With a sigh Ricard pulled his typewriter towards him and rolled in the sheet that he had last used. He had to re-type large parts of the report and it was getting late already. But even as the keys began to rattle away, he still mused about the problem of Madame Delain, and in the back of his mind he could hear an echo of Lieutenant Vellard's mysterious reference to Deschaves. He took a swig of his coffee and concentrated firmly on his work.

He awoke the next morning to the sound of heavy rain on the corrugated iron of the roof, and pains in his shoulders and back from the long hours of typing. His head was thick and his report was hanging from the wall in its tough canvas bag. The typing had been frustrating and slow, with ribbons running out at crucial moments. He recalled that at that moment he had never wanted to have to write another report in his life. And he had dreamed, he thought, about that annoying troublemaker, Vellard.

Yet as he walked onto the parade ground with rain streaming down his face and into the weighty fabric of his greatcoat, as he surveyed the shivering, hollow faces of those men not on duty or suffering from the week's bout of dysentery, or even the dreaded flu, and saw their pathetically futile attempts to look like soldiers in the face of mud and wet and hard work, he was in a surprisingly good mood. He had had a feeling since he woke up that today his job would be easier.

Something would happen to make sense of, or solve, one of the baffling problems that beset him. The thought pleased him enormously. For a start, he told himself, there was Lieutenant Jannert, on crutches admittedly, but up out of his bed for the morning parade and saluting his major with what seemed to be a wistful air. Ricard ignored the memory of his discomfiture the day before and concentrated his mind on the positive aspect, that Jannert would be performing his duties again today – conscientiously, of course.

On the other hand, Lieutenant Vellard was still confined, and Captain Deschaves still did not look as though a smile would ever again disrupt his prematurely ageing features. Ricard's good mood was undaunted. He even gave a brief impromptu talk to the soldiers, urging them not to be disheartened and praising them for the hard work they had done. Some scowled at him as he spoke, but others looked genuinely pleased, and Ricard sensed that his good mood had spread, which he found gratifying.

He exchanged a few words with Deschaves and finalised the arrangements for the day. The captain was to continue his investigation into the causes of the small outbreak of dysentery among the troops. Ricard had been apprehensive about giving him the duty – a little below a captain's status, he felt, but the captain had practically volunteered. This meant, however, that there were no officers to oversee the work on the battlefield – except Ricard. He had not particularly wanted to do this because it took him away from his central position in the village, but today he was happy to. The details were lined up and fallen out. They filed off through the lessening rain.

There had been some debate in his mind about what to do with Jannert – he couldn't despatch him to the battlefield with his injured leg, and there wasn't much to be done in the village other than receive the repetitive reports of the details sent to seek out Madame Delain unless some emergency arose. So he left him to do as he pleased and to "generally keep the place tidy". Implicit in that was the role of keeping an eye on Vellard, but that did not appear to present many problems. It seemed that there was nothing more to be done within the bounds of the new Pericard. Everything was ordered as close to how it should be as possible, and what required ordering had to be followed out on to the mass of earth and ruins to the east of the huddled collection of buildings.

The mud was deeper and stickier today than it usually was – the rain had made it the consistency of wet plaster. Ricard found it hard to struggle through and the water running down the back of his neck had lost the exhilarating freshness it had had when he had first noticed it on the parade ground. His good mood still remained nonetheless. He met the first group of soldiers not far from the communications trench where the helmets and rifles still kept their watch for the dead men. On his way there he had caught a brief glimpse of the dull metal of the first few of them, but had resolutely looked away and not thought about them. Their gloomy silence did not fit with his present state of mind.

The soldiers carefully avoided clearing debris from too close to that sacred ground. Instead, the drift of their movement was away from it, deeper into the old no man's land, closer to the old German trenches, which had so far been left undisturbed. Ricard watched them patiently as they struggled with larger pieces of rubbish.

The only sounds were of the rain dripping steadily on Ricard's already sodden clothes and into black puddles and the quiet swearing of men as they pulled on rough metal edges with bruised fingers. When things were eventually yanked out of the mire they emerged with a sucking groan and the underground stench of rotting flesh, human and animal, would belch out of the cut earth and make men turn their heads away.

It was so painfully slow and continually dangerous for all of them that Ricard felt his cheerfulness ebbing. With it went a heightened sense in him that he had only become aware of because it was going. He couldn't identify it exactly so he put it down to the strong hold his sleep still had over him. He concentrated hard on the physical details of what was going on in front of him. He flicked water that had gathered on his moustache out on to the mud in great silvery globules. He supposed, as another waft of turtle-smell brushed over him, that he had been wrong in his bright expectations that morning. When he returned across the wasteland to his cold hut nothing would have changed. Everything would still be as tangled and silently dangerous as the long rusted lines of barbed wire between the two sets of trenches. He sighed, and decided that the grey-blue of this clearing party was beginning to become embedded the backs of his eyes.

He beckoned the sergeant in charge over and began to explain his plan of action; that he was off to observe the second clearing party, then the third, and ultimately come back to this one. He added that the sergeant should send for him at either of these two places if any emergencies arose.

As he spoke he saw the man's eyes begin to gaze idly behind him. Then they widened suddenly and as the skin stretched around them it stretched around the mouth as well and a hand pointed eagerly beyond Ricard's shoulder. As Ricard turned, abandoning his dignity in a moment of overwhelming curiosity, the sergeant wailed in a high voice:

"It's Madame Delain!"

Ricard's feet were uncertain on the slippery earth. He almost knocked the diminutive sergeant to the ground by swinging a hand to balance himself. But the man was right.

She was smeared from head to foot in the stinking grime. Her hair and what was left of her clothes were so plastered to her body that she seemed rather to be made out of the mud than to be human. She had climbed out of the memorial trench, it seemed, because she stood on the very edge of it, where the black earth had been raised in the war to protect heads from explosions. Her feet churned the liquid ground as she swayed to and fro, always threatening to return to the subterranean muck from which she had come. She did not put out her arms to balance herself but clutched them to her shoulders.

She must be cold.

The thought darted between all of Ricard's other emotions as he stared at the apparition. It was her. She looked so alien, but he did not for a second doubt the sergeant's cry. It was Madame Delain, and she had returned. Every second, though, she threatened to depart again, permanently. She still risked slipping backwards into the trench.

Ricard overcame his sense of shock and began to inch forward carefully. He gestured behind him for the others to stay where they were. He did not want to startle her. Nor did he want to take his eyes off her in case in such a half-moment she slipped at last. It was laborious to creep forward through that mud and not make any sudden movements. It felt a long time even before he could see her face behind its mask. His heart shuddered in the confines of his chest even more than the muscles in his legs. If his lips had not been moistened by the water that ran from his face and moustache he would barely have been able to speak his first careful words to her.

"Madame Delain! Don't move! I'll come to you."

He gradually removed his greatcoat as he got nearer to her. He could see that she was shivering uncontrollably. He barely breathed. He could feel shell cases hard under his feet, and more yielding things that he did not dare think about.

At last he was within touching distance of her. He looked up from his position on the decaying sandbags slightly below her and, as if for the first time ever her eyes, white against the grey-black of the mud on her skin, moved in his direction. He made as if to approach again, more careful words forming in the back of his throat. But as the muscles in his arm tensed to reach out to her they did no more than brush her skin. Her body lurched from the brink of the trench, over the short stretch of earth and down into him. Her head lolled over his shoulder, the wind shot out of his lungs, but he caught her. Out of the corner of his eye he saw the sergeant and the other men rushing to take the cold limbs from his embrace. As soon as he could speak again he was mixing comforting words with orders directed over the emaciated shoulders resting on his chest.

"We'll take you back now, you'll be warm – Sergeant! Pick up my coat and put it on her shoulders – you'll be warm, you can rest."

He could feel her cold breath on his neck.

Celine

Five days passed in which the intensity of each touch, each kindly word was dragged out in an eagerness to taste every last fragment of pleasure, dragged out so far that their value became bitter, as though their final days together had become the dregs of happiness that they had to drink.

Now her body was tired but she carried on. She moved continuously between piles of clothes – one on the bed, the other, smaller, in the case on the floor – picking, comparing, discarding and putting certain items on the smaller pile. She smoothed these things down very carefully, but her movements were never deliberate. She seemed to throw things down without a glance, then examine others for several minutes at a time. In all her turning and lifting and placing and smoothing she never found a second to wipe the running stream of tears on her cheeks. She simply carried on, only frowning when a wayward splash dampened the clothes chosen for the pile in the case. Barely a thought crossed her mind for hours. She was swallowed up in an awareness, a consistent knowledge that he was going in two days. And she had wasted that time...

She paused. His hands were around her waist and his nose was nuzzling the back of her neck.

"Don't keep doing that, my love. You know they will not allow me to take everything." His voice grew even softer. "Let me do it. Don't worry, I'll take what's important. Look."

She turned and glanced over his face before seeing what he held in his strong fingers. It was a photograph of her. A bolt of anguish shot through her body. How could she have turned from him for those weeks? And now he would be taken from her in two days. "Don't cry, don't cry. I won't be gone for that long. Not for very long. And I'm here with you now. I am coming back…"

That wasted time! She would never forgive herself. Even now his voice seemed to be fading. Desperately, she reached out for him and her hands caught hold of his clothes. She could feel his flesh, so familiar, beneath the cloth. She would do anything to have him here for ever. As she embraced him and buried her face in the front of his shirt she demanded that God would grant her wish.

It was an unexpected sense of happiness that she awoke to. Happiness tinged with other things, mostly sadness at the sudden loss of Major Villier's understanding, but happiness nonetheless. Lieutenant Vellard was wrong after all. The major could understand loss, even if only a little. She had sensed it draining out of him as she had teetered on the edge of the trench. Unlike Captain Deschaves, though, his loss of understanding was painless because he barely knew he had it. There was still the odd sensation of being a centre of fascination, at least, in a quarter where she had not really expected such a thing. It was not an unwelcome discovery but she would have been horrified by any idea that his feelings might be reciprocated. They were not, of course. She was sure of that.

Her mind wandered in this limbo of reflection while the events of the past week, a week which had been in itself a sort of limbo, drifted to and fro on the edge of her mental scope. At the moment no firm memories made themselves known. Only the faintest impression of her husband's fingers remained on her skin. Into the bubble of private space in which she floated came a shape which seemed to speak, asking her if she needed anything.

"No, thank you, I'm fine."

She could tell she was mumbling the words but the sensation of her lips seemed apart from the thoughts that urged them to move. In fact the physical world was more distant than she ever remembered. She could not even tell what she was lying on, and the building in which she lay did not appear to be solid, more a shifting collection of features. The person, whoever it was, was speaking again, but the words were a jumble, as though her ears were too disdainful to trouble themselves with mere sounds.

"I don't know. Let me rest."

She thought she saw the figure's shoulders droop. It went away from her. It seemed like the major. Perhaps it was. It should be, he was thinking a lot about her, she knew that.

There was still the problem of Lieutenant Vellard and Captain Deschaves. This thought came strongly into her head and made ripples that disturbed the serene surface of the things she had thought and the things she had felt. The ripples did not go, and she could no longer see the major's worried face in her mind so clearly. But she could not smooth them. She felt as though she should be able to glide easily to him, or to Lieutenant Vellard, while she lay there but she could not. The world was only what was in her mind at that moment. She suspected that what she remembered would still exist, but she was unsure. Only the ripples were distinct. She hoped that they were not all that remained. She drifted again and even the ripples grew distinct from her.

"I am coming back, very soon." He smiled. She tried hard to believe him.

The second awakening was different. Memories of the

first remained but now memories of her time in the trenches overlaid them, solid and sharp as crystal. The major was beside her – she was certain of that this time, but between the two of them stretched the ranks of dead men and their reasons.

The landscape over which Jean-Paul had led her was very different from the one she had been used to. The new village had faded out of sight almost instantly and, as if to compensate, the raised parts of the battlefield had risen up higher. Out of them protruded gleaming metal and dull flesh. The air was dank with a hint of burning around it. Over the trenches and out in no man's land a pall of smoke, or gas, or something, hung, a white mass.

Jean-Paul led her into the mass to a place where the barbed wire still rested on steel supports. There too sandbags were still carefully piled around the lips of trenches, and from sentry posts rifles and machine guns were still trained on the low lines of sandbags that, half covered by mist, marked the silent German lines. Jean-Paul led her along the top of one of these trenches. She looked down and she could see men at their posts or huddling against the boards that held the walls of each trench up out of the damp air below. Some held cards in their hands. Others just sat and stared. It was these men who looked up as she passed, sometimes tilting back battered helmets to get a clearer view. She avoided their eyes when this happened. Jean-Paul still held her hand and still kept her in his sight, which was reassuring, but she was afraid.

When at length he turned to her and whispered that they had come to the right place even his immediate reassurance had lessened. She was startled to see that after three years in the trenches he did not look that different from the incarnation of him dead that she was used to. Now she knew why he had not come home on leave.

"Ladder there!"

A ladder was pulled by two shambling men from a place at the foot of the trench's firestep and put up on the other side, just beneath where her feet rested on top of the line of sandbags. She saw Jean-Paul motion the men to turn away. Then he offered his thin, pale hand to help her on to the wooden steps. The ladder was not safe, sometimes just held together by wire. She clutched her skirts close about her as she made her slow way down. For a second she stood in the strangely warm but half-dark trench alone. Then Jean-Paul came down and stood beside her with a welcoming smile on his lips. He ran his hands down her arms affectionately.

"I had to bring you here. I'm sorry, but I had to."

He turned to one side and spoke quickly and quietly to a very young-looking man who was staring at her with blue eyes. There was a broad smear of crisped mud across his white forehead. He took his gaze from her with difficulty, but mumbled something and hurried along the sinking duckboards round a sharp corner in the line of the trench.

As he went Jean-Paul took her hand again and led her out of the immediate circle of staring eyes, soaking uniforms, bags of grenades and tin mugs of bitter-smelling coffee. That circle was replaced by another, and another, and another as they went along the sharply delineated blast protection that disrupted the trench's line.

Every now and then there were some variations on the scene – a few tins of food were clutched in bony fingers, men's coats were replaced by sodden blankets, there were open wounds which gave off the stink of gangrene, there were games of chess, there were rats. Overall though most of what she saw did not change dramatically. Always thin, hopeless faces, always wide, fascinated eyes. She was afraid of them but she stared back with a similar fascination. These were the dead of Pericard, still on duty years after some of them had died and months after the end of the war had permitted their living comrades to go home to poverty and the Spanish flu in the rest of France.

One other detail caught her eye. Here and there in the eerily still and silent clusters of staring men were figures whose uniforms – somehow – were a deeper blue than the others', whose faces were less lined and dirty and who did not peer out from under helmet rims but had unbowed heads and could look at her fully. She walked closer to Jean-Paul and pressed the wasted muscles of his hand more tightly.

The walk along the trench seemed to last a long time, but eventually Jean-Paul stopped in front of a low doorway in the rear side of the trench over which hung a brown curtain made heavy by the damp.

"We shall just wait here for a few minutes. If you don't mind, that is."

He squeezed her shoulder as he spoke and she felt a tingling in her arms and chest that urged her to embrace him and feel his body wasted and thin through the stiff material of his uniform. But she could not under the apparently lidless eyes of the five or six men that stood or sat around the mysterious doorway cleaning rust-covered riles or scraping mud off discoloured bayonets. She pressed her arms around herself and tried not to think of how his warm breath would be in her hair if it was not so severely tied back. The feeling lessened but it did not go away.

He smiled at her sheepishly but only asked if she was cold and offered his stained and splitting coat. It had his warmth in it as she put it round her shoulders. That seeped into her skin but could not dissipate the burning of tears in her throat. Her thoughts were building up to a pitch of fear and frustration in her head, but then they were interrupted.

"Private Dessons wanted to come and see you."

He was still as shy as he had been in life, and he still tilted his head to one side as he spoke. His deferential words barely reached her ears but they still provoked a slight trickling of tears from her eyes.

"I've done what you told me, Madame Delain, I've looked after Lieutenant Delain. And my parents are coming soon so I can be buried properly like Lieutenant Delain. I just wanted you to know that I've done what I was told."

He looked up at Jean-Paul as he faltered to a stop to see that his words were approved. Jean-Paul nodded to him and granted him a brief smile. The boy saluted and took a couple of bashful steps backwards, his rifle banging against his thigh as he did so. She looked at him for a long time and then switched her gaze back to her husband, who was looking between them proudly as he might have done if they were a family. Then he gathered himself again and Private Dessons disappeared in to the background. Jean-Paul cleared his throat.

"Well now, I think I'd better introduce you to some of the officers."

He pulled back the curtain and ushered her down creaking wooden steps into a thick atmosphere filled with lamp oil, tobacco fumes and male sweat, not to mention urine that seemed to have soaked through the soft mud walls of the dugout. In the strong orange light four silhouettes moved in surprise from their positions round a table to greet them. Jean-Paul saluted and introduced her. Then, as her eyes got used to the light and the stinging caused by the air, he pointed out each of them and gave them names.

"Lieutenant Leclerc – Lieutenant Bonnard – Captain Melion – Lieutenant Deladdier."

There was almost a hush in his voice as he pronounced the last name and the breath of it brushed across her cheek.

Lieutenant Deladdier extended a hand towards her. As he moved she could see a crucifix on the wall behind him. By the time they had finished their greetings her eyes were used to the light and her lungs to the air. She took the chair that was offered and began to study her surroundings with great interest. Here and there on the walls were pictures. She saw her own, and understood that some of them were of those left behind. There was a Monet card that she recognised, and some others. There were a few books on a makeshift earth shelf, their covers growing white mould. On the table there was a chessboard with chessmen crudely shaped out of wood and a field telephone. The receiver hung limply on its cable close to the floor.

The four men were hardly different from the soldiers outside except for the pistols on their belts and their epaulettes. She put her hand on the table and her fingers encountered crumpled paper and cold metal. It was a small package of the tokens used during rationing instead of the old coins. She pushed it away from her and turned her attention again to Lieutenant Deladdier. It was hard to ignore him – he had the deeper blue and the stronger face of those occasional men she had seen outside. All the other officers seemed to be pressed aside by him, though his movements were unobtrusive and careful.

"Welcome to our trench, Madame Delain."

His voice was low and cultured. He was clean-shaven and his eyes loomed out from below large eyebrows.

"Thank you sir."

Lieutenant Deladdier laughed in a guttural choking way.

"Don't call me sir. Has Lieutenant Delain not told you who I am?"

"No."

"Sorry. I should have done, I suppose. Lieutenant Deladdier was in command in the church in Pericard.

When the walls fell in – you know the story."

"That was me. You will have seen my men outside."

She could feel Jean-Paul's hand on her shoulder as she had done so many times. This time it sent a shiver through her body but she drew courage from the familiar sensation.

"I'm very honoured to meet you. You are a mysterious figure."

"Don't stand up please. It is no honour to meet me. You and your husband have enough honour between you."

"But I suppose I've been brought here for a reason. I have enough reason to be here in my Jean-Paul, but you haven't brought Anne or Marie or the others who have similar reasons."

As she spoke she raised her own hand up to her shoulder and placed it on Jean-Paul's. She felt his fingers tighten in a surreptitious caress.

"No, I haven't brought them, and yes, I did have a specific reason for bringing you. You must take some news back to Pericard. What that news is we don't, I'm afraid, quite know yet. But it is of great importance."

"Why have you brought me then? Surely it would be best to tell Lieutenant Vellard. It might even calm him."

Lieutenant Deladdier smiled sadly.

"If it were that simple that's what we would have done. But we must keep you here for a few days. By that time you will understand more fully than anyone else left in the world what Major Villier and Lieutenant Vellard really mean to us. But now…"

"A few days! They will search for me. And the warrant! He won't stop it will he?"

"I don't think they will find you here. And as for the warrant – do you really believe Major Villier will allow it to be stopped?"

There was a calm that emanated from Lieutenant Deladdier and from everything around him, even the weapons that he and his companions carried in their belts. She felt her objections calming under its influence and that of Jean-Paul's presence. She watched Lieutenant Deladdier watch her subside into a quiet posture on the chair. She saw a glint in his eyes as he looked away that spoke of a man who had been dryly witty before the church had fallen on him and his comrades and turned them into the guardians of Pericard. He was smiling when he spoke again.

"Now, I understand what it is to miss your family. I think, Captain and Lieutenants, that we should perhaps leave the lieutenant and Madame Delain alone for a time."

She looked up and saw Jean-Paul flush red.

"Thank you, Lieutenant Deladdier."

He pointed a grimy finger at a curled family photograph next to an old calendar on the wall.

"It was my son's sixteenth birthday last week. I know what it's like to be apart, my dear."

He smiled at her again and led the other officers out into the grey trench. Jean-Paul stroked her forehead in the muggy smelly air before bending down to kiss her.

"Madame Delain?"

She shot through layers of remembrance and opened her eyes suddenly into the face of the major. He looked a little startled by her sudden awakening, but recovered himself quickly and remembered to turn his worried expression into a more gentle and comforting one. Even so, she was ashamed to have him here. She wasn't sure why. Perhaps it was his proximity to her thoughts of Jean-Paul. He seemed to be going on with a conversation. Perhaps she had been answering even before she knew she was with him.

"Thank goodness you've woken up. You've been asleep for a long time. I just came – really – to reassure you. To tell you not to worry about the warrant. That's not been delayed or affected."

"Thank you sir. What day is it?"

She was surprised that her voice came out as a croak. Her throat did not feel sore – but then she could not feel her body very much at all. She had been used to that before she went out to the trenches, but there she had learned to appreciate sensations again.

She tried to see the major better but it was too hard and she lay back down.

"It is Friday, Madame."

"Friday!"

She was aware of her hand flying out and grasping hold of something warm. After a few seconds she realised that it was the major's hand and he was looking from it to her with some alarm. She let go.

"I've slept for two days!"

"Well, not exactly Madame. You have been ill – it is only to be expected – but even so, you can remember the date. Your mind is very resilient."

She lay back and closed her eyes. She wasn't sure why she had panicked. Perhaps the seriousness on Lieutenant Deladdier's kindly face as he imparted his news to her had thrown her into a state of terrible urgency. But there was no real hurry. The message was important, certainly, but there was time enough for her to regain some strength so that she could communicate it properly. She relaxed. If she opened her eyelids just a fraction she could see the major bending intently over her. She could feel the warmth of his hand next to her neck on the pillow. It reminded her of Jean-Paul's warmth but it was not close enough to that to deceive her.

"I'm awake, sir. Please carry on. I'm very tired though."

Before she closed her eyes fully again she saw him

step back quickly and pull his hand away from her to a pocket in his uniform jacket. She could just about hear the breath he took when he was back on his seat and about to begin talking again.

"Lieutenant Georges did say that I was not to bother you for too long, so I'll be gone in a moment. I just wanted to add that the Regimental Headquarters in Rheims have told me, this morning, that your warrant and those of the others are, I quote, 'very far advanced'."

"Is that good news?"

"I don't know whether answers will be negative or positive. But whatever they are they'll be here soon. Perhaps as early as Monday. Perhaps not for two weeks."

"It will be a relief to Anne and Marie – and to me. This is very quick. I'd expected to wait months."

The major coughed in an embarrassed way. She heard him moving about on his seat.

"There are people at Rheims who – will listen to my suggestions. Don't worry – nobody has been compromised. You have benefited from my doing it."

"I see. In that case thank you again."

"Well – I can see you are tired. I shall go. Get some rest."

"Goodbye sir. Thank you for what you've done."

Then he was gone. Celine lay on the bed in an agony of feelings. If the warrant came and it said yes she would go immediately, take Jean-Paul and go. If it said no – she preferred not to think of that. But this would mean abandoning them all. Loyalties tugged at her – Lieutenant Deladdier, Anne, Marie, even Major Villier. She had to fulfil her obligations, make everyone understand. What if it came on Monday? The time spent in the hot fog of the dugout reached over her and she decided. She would do what Jean-Paul wanted. Under the sheet her legs turned and twisted.

The days in the trenches had been long ones. At first Jean-Paul had hardly let her out beyond the heavy gas curtain for fear of the effect she would produce on the filthy miserable men outside and vice versa. But she had explained that she needed to see in order to be able to convince the people of Pericard, and, as he had always done before the war, he let her have her way. She spent hour after hour wandering between the men in the rain, a thin figure between wide greatcoats and blankets shrugged around shoulders.

It was usually quiet in the trenches, but this quiet was not like the silence over the battlefield she knew. That silence was one of exhaustion as though some great creature had thrashed in agony for so long it had worn itself out. Here, the silence was one of expectation. Men went about with half an eye always watching the parapet, and spoke to her in an almost distracted way. It was only when she tried to go from the second-line trench to the front-line ones along the communication line that she knew had memorials to these men lying at its base, and was stopped firmly but politely that she realised why.

"Can't go down there I'm afraid Madame."

"Why?"

Private Dessons' face was almost incredulous. He looked at her as though she was mad, but did his best to be patient.

"It's dangerous Madame. Only the forward companies are allowed down there. Lieutenant would never forgive me."

After this she began to understand. The fact that men would disappear and be replaced by others who slept and did not speak for a day. The fact that officers would be seen talking intently with each other, or would disappear themselves. The fact that men still cleaned their rifles and kept them loaded. The fact that no-one ever climbed on to the firestep and peered over the parapet except the sentries. These men were still fighting the war.

They were still occupying ground recaptured from the enemy – the trench she stood in was an old front-line one adapted to give support to the one in front. Deprived of life and purpose by the war, its ending had severed them a second time from what they knew and understood. They were trapped in a limbo, unable to go home, unable to defeat the enemy because he was no longer there.

In the new Pericard they kept the links with home and families alive through the villagers and the garrison. Here in the trenches that surrounded and ran through the old Pericard they lived the only life that had been given to them since their enlistment, the only existence that made sense to men who had been sucked into the stinking mud and cold metal. Home was a fantasy – they only touched it in dreams. Reality was the war, and so in the reality they made after death they made a war so that thousands could live less well than beasts but still be on the only earth they could remember.

Now she believed the apparently impossible stories she had always heard about the day of the Armistice. On being asked if they had cheered that November morning, men returning from the front had looked blankly at their questioners. No-one had cheered, they said. The guns had stopped and for a while men had just stared in a daze at mud or Germans or each other. Without the war there was no meaning any more. It was only afterwards that families and love had even begun to take on any importance in their lives again.

That was why, she grasped suddenly, she had had to come to the front herself. Jean-Paul wanted concrete evidence that there was another world, not just a bright thing he visited in dreams. She could have sent a messenger, but he would not have come back unless she herself came to show him her own reality. She prayed that Jean-Paul *could* finally be freed – she had never doubted it before, but now she was close to him and his comrades. In Pericard it was the lives that the men never lived that mattered. In the trenches it was the lives that they had been forced to live. The two did not seem to be able to co-exist, but as she got to know the soldiers she began to realise that the men existed in what they understood but prayed for that which they could never directly experience.

These realisations were the work of one or two days, but when they were complete she began to see the consequences in every man's face, especially Jean-Paul's. It hurt her to see that the embarrassment she had seen in him in front of the other officers was not modesty as she had thought, but in fact the discomfort of a man who has proved the impossible. She was very real to him, but at the same time completely unbelievable, a dream to be treasured, but also to be kept secure and distant in case it was contaminated or itself contaminated what was real. That was why she had been stared at so intently when she had arrived. Her awareness of it doubled the peculiarity of the conversations she had had with the men. There were often long discussions in which they revealed all that they had dreamed of for home, but the way they spoke always reminded her that home and she herself were only dreams. She had to touch her own hands to stay in contact with the reality of the trench.

Private Dessons, of course, did not feel this. He had barely fought and had lived long enough to see the gloomy Christmas that the war was over by. She drew closer to the boy, her "nephew" she called him, half seriously. In the days when Jean-Paul seemed to be on the other side of a bridge even longer than that she perceived between herself and Major Villier she would seek him out. When he was not on sentry duty she would take comfort in his knowledge of the things he now dreamed about. After these conversations she would always go back to Jean-Paul with eagerness because the bridge seemed, briefly, to have been crossed.

"What does Lieutenant Vellard know about you? He refuses to be a part of what Major Villier wants to do, you know."

"Lieutenant Vellard..."

Private Dessons laughed a little sheepishly and a nervous chuckle ran round the lips of the men around them.

"Lieutenant Vellard should be here. Everything he had before the war – and it was little enough, if what we've been told is true – he has lost. There was no mercy for him. He is the only survivor out of all his brothers and of his company who fought at the Somme. He lost everything, and it left him thinking about nothing else but the war. Because of this he – he feels all the things we – these men – felt in the war and feel now. His head's open to all of it. He understands every bit of what we think. It is as though he has a telephone line into the trenches."

The soldier who spoke was one of Pericard's twelve ghostly defenders. His heavy-looking face was thoughtful.

"There's nothing left of him in the world except his body. Otherwise he is still fighting. He's like us – the only person who is, in your Pericard. So he feels all our pain of being wounded and cold and getting ill. It all goes through him. We feel everything that he experiences. But it is spread out amongst us, and is less intense. He is the only channel for what we feel – well, you must have seen the consequences. You saw, the last time it all went off in him. Everyone else feels our joy or excitement, which we always put in the same places as our thoughts of home – that's why you feel it, see?"

The soldier leaned on the butt of his rifle and pursed

his lips. Others looked away, embarrassed. Celine shook her head at the difficulty of it all. She had never realised just how much more Lieutenant Vellard had understood. She had just thought he was misguided.

"Can Lieutenant Vellard be right then?"

"He is, but so is Major Villier. Lieutenant Vellard wants the war to go on for ever like we do – it is the only way we will get to be who we were. In real life we are only the war, aren't we? Major Villier wants to erase it, to tidy it up and start things going again. We sort of want to – at least, we know it's got to happen. Lieutenant Vellard don't see it because he's in the wrong place. You, though, you see…"

Here the soldier jabbed a stocky finger at her. His jowls shook as he emphasised his words. He slid his dull grey eyes to the right for a second and then looked back at her.

"You and the others have the hardest job, I reckon. You have to live our lives for us. Lieutenant Vellard sees people as they were. Major Villier isn't bothered with them. You have to deal with folks who never were, but who might have been lots of different people."

The soldier let his eyes drop from her face. She stared at his forehead for a second, surprised by the eloquence. She had never known anyone try to explain things so complex in such a structured way, and it was especially remarkable in a soldier who, from what he said, had only learned to read "by accident". She glanced to the soldier's right as these thoughts ran through her mind and saw the uniforms of Lieutenant Deladdier and Jean-Paul just slipping out of sight. The soldier, looking up again, just shrugged and mumbled something about "they being taught to put it all in words". Private Dessons looked ashamed. He had been an accomplice.

They were feeding her knowledge. She thought she

146

should have been offended but... She was curious. That evening she held back from Jean-Paul's embrace and demanded to be told what was going on. She acted more anger than she felt – it was impossible to be furious with the needs of these shrunken, pale men. But to her horror Jean-Paul's face ran with sudden tears.

"Please don't misunderstand me. Please, I beg of you Celine. I'm doing what's right. It's important for us all. You must understand as much as you can."

He was practically sobbing at her feet. She began to feel like a child who, without thinking, had rejected the affection of a parent. Images of their life together swam in her head. She bent down and kissed his hot face.

"Why didn't you just tell me?"

He raised a trembling hand and put it on her chest next to her heart.

"How much of me do you really know? How much of me do you absolutely trust?"

She knew the answer should be "All of you" but in addressing that to him she was talking to the husband she had waved off on the train. Since then she had had letters and visitations but not him, not until now. Still – she owed it to the man she had bid farewell to trust him as he was now.

"We all have to tell you because we are all together now. Each of us has a role to play now. We all have to fit together in the trenches. Like Private Minon said, you have to look after us that might have been, the us you knew. We only remember them, just like you do. Oh, I can't explain it any more. I love you, I always have done, but the man you take home in the coffin will be the man who was used to waking up next to you. I will be the man who remembers a sensation like being used to waking up next to you."

He clasped his arms round her legs and ground his forehead into her knees. The feeling of the scraping he gave to his skin sent shudders through her. She understood the causes now, but the reality of his despair was out of her reach. Major Villier did not understand her loss; she did not understand Jean-Paul's. They knew the facts; they could not feel them.

Two days later Lieutenant Deladdier had approached her in the dugout with his cap in his hand. Both Jean-Paul and Private Dessons had gone to the front line. She had sat curled up on Jean-Paul's bunk sniffing the leaden air of the dugout and feeling the drab mud walls begin to creep behind her eyes.

"Excuse me. I hope I'm not disturbing you."

"No, not at all. I'm already pretty disturbed."

"I'm sorry. But you understand us now, don't you? You understand everything."

"Do I? …What happens to the trenches at the border with Switzerland? What happens to the trenches when they reach the sea?"

Lieutenant Deladdier nodded slowly as though he'd been waiting for the question. He pulled a chair over and sat down opposite her.

"When the trenches reach Switzerland there is a great cliff. And the trenches fall off into space. At the coast the trenches go under the water and the men fought in diving suits. Some are there still, being eaten by fishes instead of rats."

He said all this with perfect seriousness. She did not know whether to believe him or not, but stared into his creased face with wide eyes. Then he allowed the faintest of mischievous smiles to cross his lips.

"The point is that it doesn't matter what happened to the trenches. To try and understand everything about the trenches is to ask too much of God. Lieutenant Jannert, for example – you know that he has resolved to leave the army? Good – still feels totally bewildered by what's happened to him, but in his soul he really understands. He's survived the war, and he's going to go home to Verdun in the place of all those who cannot go home. He knows that he has to live for the ones who are dead. That is exactly what we ultimately ask of everyone in Pericard. On the other hand think of Captain Deschaves. You have been given more than him. God only gives enough understanding to keep us sane and to keep us believing in him. Be satisfied. You understand Pericard. That is enough."

"Everything except why all this has happened here."

"I had a lot of faith in the time before, you know, the time before the war. As the church wall collapsed on me I begged God to give me more life so I could come to him more pure. We prayed as we died… And God granted our wishes – in a way. I suppose it proves that there's irony in heaven. After what happened to us men kept praying for our intercession, for us to help them gain their wishes. They left their offerings to God in the shrines and after the war they left their thanks to us in the trench with the rifles and helmets. We do not deserve it but it is better to be remembered like that than just to be a story. One day, I suppose, we will not even be that, for all Lieutenant Vellard can do. I'm afraid my explanation of 'why' is perhaps not clear. But Pericard is special. Even those who died in other places on the front don't have the understanding we do. Let us pray God granted them peace. But I've gone on quite enough, I'm sure. My chief errand to you is, as I'm suppose you will expect, connected to what I have told you. I must get onto it."

So the "news" was to come now. She had expected more ceremony. But Lieutenant Deladdier looked very serious.

Cries and shouts. Their urgency spurred a fear of creeping danger into her and she covered the exposed parts of her neck with the blanket so that the warmth would give the illusion of safety. She could feel fear in the village and a deep well of anger that had suddenly burst out and taken hold of all weak feelings. The fear grew and was painful.

Someone was crying outside and Celine's face too was tear-stained. She knew she could not walk far enough to offer help, but she tried to feel strong for the woman or boy who was unable to cope. There was a commotion at the door. It rattled and there were loud shouts – almost overwhelming – sounding aggressive on the other side. As boots clumped across the boards of the other room Celine shrank below her blanket as if by making herself small enough she might not be seen.

The people in the other room were angry and upset. Their minds were so perplexed that she could not even guess at who they were. They sounded heavy-footed as though they were carrying something. The noises stopped for a moment but the emotions on the other side of the door remained high.

All at once there was a voice issuing instructions, more footsteps and the door crashed open under the weight of a soldier's shoulder. He was carrying a stretcher. The second soldier followed him, and then Lieutenant Georges and Major Villier. The figure on the stretcher was unloaded onto the bed and for a few moments Lieutenant Georges fussed around it. It groaned with the voice of Captain Deschaves. Major Villier was practically jumping around in a fury but he did still find time to apologise to her for the interruption and to assure her that she would be well guarded.

"Why? What's happening?"

"Lieutenant Vellard. He's escaped, severely injured Captain Deschaves and taken some men with him."

"What?"

This time Major Villier cut in before Lieutenant Georges could continue his explanation.

"Vellard has made a break for it. He and some other mutineers have made for the battlefield. He overpowered the sentry, don't ask me what the sentry was doing inside the hut, took his weapon and shot Captain Deschaves even though the captain was talking to me and not trying to stop him. But, Madame Delain, do not fear. I have suspended all the work on the battlefield and have deployed the garrison defensively. We outnumber him, and as soon as we identify where he is hiding we shall not hesitate to surround and capture – or kill – him. Your safety, Madame, is not in question."

Celine nodded but could not summon the spirit to make a reply. She knew why Vellard had decided to escape. As for capturing him – she did not think that that option would be available to anyone who attacked him. Perhaps something could be done still, but not by her. Not yet, at least. Poor Captain Deschaves! Lieutenant Vellard's hate had found physical expression as well as spiritual.

In the long silence that followed the major's departure Celine measured and contemplated the things she could feel in the village. Everyone knew that something was about to change dramatically. This was a consequence of Lieutenant Vellard's escape. No-one knew what the change was but they all feared it – another consequence. Celine feared it too, though she knew that what the others feared had no connection with what she was to tell them. They had to understand before it took place, or…

She pushed herself up on her elbows and looked across the dim chamber at the hunched form of Captain Deschaves. He had been awake – she had heard him mutter two or three times. He was not feverish either – the invectives against Lieutenant Vellard had been too bitter for that.

She slipped quietly out of bed and moved quickly over the rough floor. The sensation of wood against her feet reminded her that she was still only wearing a thin underdress but she suspected that Captain Deschaves was in no state even to be aware of her lack of modesty. She crouched by his bed and tapped with one finger against his cheek. At last his eyes opened reluctantly and a kind of fitful consciousness came over him. At first he clutched at his shoulder instinctively but when the initial shock of pain was over the pupils of his blue-ringed eyes rolled over towards her. As they focussed they closed. A shuddering breath went through him.

"Go away."

"I'm not responsible for Lieutenant Vellard. But I do know why…"

"Go away."

"You said to me 'what happens to the trenches when they reach Switzerland or the sea?' I didn't know then but I do now."

"I don't care. Go away."

"We will all lose what you lost. They're all going. Lieutenant Vellard wants to go with them."

"What about Captain Deschaves? Why is he different from the rest of us? You've been hinting all these things about him. It must be important."

Jean-Paul straightened up from his crouch next to the stove in the dugout. He had restored his uniform to a roughly presentable state and was attempting to get some more heat into the room when her question caught him unawares. It shouldn't have, she thought. She was always asking him questions now, especially since he usually appeared to answer eagerly. It reminded them of conversations at home, now long ago in their minds, and seemed to bring them together over the void made by the war. But this time he coughed nervously before speaking.

"It is a rather delicate matter... I wouldn't want to go into details..."

"Jean-Paul! You want me to trust you. I want some confidence in return."

He sighed and faced her. She smiled up at him and he sat down beside her on the rumpled bed.

"You know Vellard and Deschaves came from the same area... Nice? You don't have to nod quite so seriously you know! Well – you know that Deschaves was a teacher – foreign languages I think – and Vellard was the youngest of four brothers?"

He laughed lightly and ran his fingers through her hair, but she could tell he didn't really want to go on. She looked expectantly at him. She wanted to hear what was behind that tension between the two officers almost as much as she wanted to hear his affectionate voice speaking to her again.

"Vellard left school and went straight into the army... He was a very quiet boy, rather sickly, but pleasant. Deschaves was his teacher... The two of them... Deschaves took Vellard rather too eagerly under his wing... you see what I mean?"

"I do. But how does that explain what's happened to the captain?"

"Well, Vellard wasn't very happy about the fact that Deschaves still treated him as a pupil. He was always sensitive and he saw it as a betrayal. When they met again, after the war he had not forgotten, though other things had obviously obscured his memory of it. Their previous relationship was not – could not be – resumed. But they couldn't pretend that nothing had happened even though they tried very hard. I suppose you might have noticed. Very soon though Vellard realised how different

Deschaves' war had been to his. You know what Vellard had lost, I suppose. And Deschaves – he had lost nothing. Only his time was wasted in the trenches. On the other hand Vellard knew his whole life had been taken from him without him even getting to die."

Jean-Paul's voice had been growing in intensity as he told his story. Celine saw the pain in his eyes and leaned closer to him so that he would be able to feel her breath on his skin. She knew that he had felt an echo of everything he described. Knowing of his distress made her tremble.

"That's it, really. Vellard's come to hate the captain, and it is within his power to do something. Not... revenge as such... Vellard isn't concerned with anything like that... but he has power to influence people. People's thoughts, you know. Not completely – as you'll see when you see Major Villier again, he doesn't run our hearts – but enough. He believes that Deschaves is not exactly the right man to receive what you have received and understood."

He stopped and stared at her. His body was cold, even in the heat from the stove. Celine rubbed his arms up and down to make the blood flow through them again, but she could not break the glassy gaze that had taken possession of his eyes. She pressed her hands to his temples and brushed her lips over his face until he returned from the strange world of another man's memories and saw her again. But even as he raised his arms to take hold of her he muttered a lament under his breath.

"Poor Vellard!"

The sentences she had spoken came out in a loose jumble but they made Captain Deschaves' eyes open wide and stare at her. He lifted his head from the pillow and she could see where folds in the cloth had made impressions on his face. He felt so weak and tired. She pitied him, but she could not comfort him – she could no longer reach him with her mind. Jean-Paul's memory allowed her to run over the room in her underclothes but not to touch another man with her hand. Even as she thought about it she recalled her husband's face as she left him again. That face had had the man of 1914 in it while the man of 1917 behind it was contemplating the return to his trench.

"Say that again."

He was sitting up now, his hand clutching at the sheets. The other in its sling twisted against his body.

"They are going. Very soon Pericard will be left alone."

Lieutenant Deladdier had used these very words as he leaned forward on the creaking chair. He had impressed upon her that she must repeat what he said to the people of Pericard accurately. That was why she had begun to use his precise words.

"So – I've given you part of your instructions. You know all that you can know. And now – this is what I am to tell you. Madame Delain, we are tired. There's no enemy to fight any more. And we do want an end to the war for us. We want to leave, soon."

His eyes shone as he gazed at her. They were wet. She didn't know for certain what he was crying for.

"The date's been chosen – ten days from now. No-one knows why. It's just like the war – there are plans we know nothing about, and orders we have to follow. They just come down and we obey. We came into this limbo of God's making from the war. In the war we must leave it. I don't know where we'll go to, even if we are able to abandon the trenches – I don't know if we can even do that. Either way, we don't think we'll have connections with you, or with Pericard any more – whatever's coming will be a big change. Major Villier will be able to clear his battlefield and Lieutenant Vellard – he will join us some day. When his time is right he'll join us, though not before.

Major Villier's world will win over his anyway. He knows this though he won't admit it and that's dangerous for him."

He let his eyes move away from hers. She sat absolutely still. He cleared his throat and looked at her again.

"No more past, except in our minds. No more war, I hope. I don't know. Perhaps, no more minds, or forgetting. But God has offered no signs. All we know is that he has answered our prayers before. He has answered yours too. You remembered us. Remember us… I'm sorry – tell them everything more clearly. Tell them we thank them."

He wiped a tear from where it had trickled onto his cheek, and covered his eyes.

She had not told the news any more clearly than Lieutenant Deladdier but Captain Deschaves understood. He lay back on the bed and looked up at the ceiling.

"Why did they take it from me first?"

She did not answer. She dared not breathe the reality of it. She could not tell that to the eyes rolled upwards to the low beams, though she was sure that if he hadn't already guessed he was capable of doing so. If he did find out, she did not want to be the carrier of such information, or to remind him of his unfortunate pupil before the image returned to his mind of its own accord. She had no doubt that it would soon enough.

She had not even told him the full story of her time in the trenches, least of all her last few minutes there when she had slipped out of Jean-Paul's embrace for the final time. In the seconds before that moment her alienation from him had faded completely. She remembered how his arms and lips had felt before the war, and could feel those arms and taste those lips again in the man who had fought. It seemed that even the light contributed to the sensation.

156

The shadows cast on his face matched the pattern she remembered from the train when he left her.

It was only when she had looked away from them that the grey light instead of sunshine reminded her that this person who had been her husband was a different man. She walked away from Captain Deschaves' bedside almost as though she was leaving Jean-Paul again. She felt the patches on her arms where Jean-Paul had gripped her grow cold. Her lips tingled with the sensation of just having parted them from his. In the blur of tears she thought she could see his sad face and stooped shoulders below the high parapet's shadow and hear the words of parting he had forced out from his emotion-cramped throat.

"Remember us. As I was, remember me."

Without seeing she put her hand out onto the bed and fell onto it, spilling sobs into her blanket for the agony of the second loss.

Deschaves

Should never have touched the boy!

He knew that, he had known it a long time, but now he knew it better than ever before. It made him writhe as though his shoulder had begun to bleed again. But the pain from that wound hurt him less than the repeated blows of realisation that he *should never have touched the boy!*

Yet he had escaped censure – perhaps the village was not so close-knit as it had liked to believe itself and it was true that no-one had seen when he had led the boy off into the countryside on hot days. He had always returned flushed and had looked around himself furtively in case a finger was pointed at him, or he glimpsed, out of the corner of his eye, someone laughing behind his hand. Nothing of that sort had ever happened and he believed himself three times lucky – the boy was beautiful; he was willing; that no-one had seen, or had said they'd seen.

He had been pleased too that the boy had grown in confidence over the long holiday and when they returned to school he expected this new-found stiffness to last. But there had been misunderstandings and he had had to use sharp words in the classroom such as he had rarely had occasion to. There was no question, of course, of the special treatment that the boy had expected. He had had to make that clear. But his affection had made him too harsh and he had been cold-shouldered and his every movement for weeks had been plagued with fear of discovery, or, even worse, of betrayal.

This never happened, but his eye was never met again by the gaze of that striking figure at the back of the class,

158

and as time passed and his friendly overtures were rejected over and over again a quiet voice began to repeat again and again that he should never have allowed himself to become involved, to give into his temptation, to let affection spoil the purity of ungratified desires. But he had been beautiful and willing; but he had not been discovered; but, but – it could not be denied. He *should never have touched the boy!*

Then the war had come. He had made a good soldier for a teacher, he thought, and he had been gratified by the respect in which his ex-colleagues held him. More importantly though the war had driven temptation to the winds. He congratulated himself on the rareness of his desires, but had to admit that they only occurred when a movement, or a light in eyes reminded him of the boy he should not have touched.

But there again the war had come to his aid. The boy had been far away from him and he had believed he had escaped the danger of discovery and the pain of rejection. The privations of the trenches had been less painful because of this, though he had tried to complain with the best of them. Sometimes he had felt vague horror at himself, this total detachment from the bleeding of the men around him, but he believed always that no fate could have been worse than that which he had been in danger of at home.

His shoulder throbbed and the walls of the trenches around him dissolved. For a few seconds he lay feeling the roughness of the covers around him and hearing only his own thoughts. Slowly, he remembered. He opened his eyes and gazed balefully at the underside of the roof. The little bastard! Little bastard! In war he had found comfort but now the boy stripped it away. How could he have been here in Pericard after all that time with his bereavements and his fervour and his knowing? He had tried to treat him with respect – but it was all too late. Good war – bad war, and a few ill-considered sharp words in the classroom…

And he had been discovered! That Delain woman must know… Major Villier? If he even suspected – the shame! His shoulder throbbed again. And how had he been exposed and shamed? Through the cruel hand of his other great fear. The boy had betrayed him. The boy had also punished him by expelling him from that exalted place where he could know more than any historian ever could about men's minds in the Great War; by very nearly expelling him from this life.

How they would laugh in the cafes in the streets around his home when they found out. "That pompous teacher – lost his head over a boy – lost all he ever had!" At this is head sank deeper into the impersonal comfort of the bed. He *should never have touched the boy!*

But then, he had never known what it was to lose a brother, or a limb to the war's grinding jaws. He had seen men die, sure enough, he had seen their pain – in fact often he had put a timely end to some sufferings while other, kinder men had looked on in horror and disgust. But he had never been interested enough to share in their pain. For him the war was freedom, a chance to become a full man again rather than a teacher who had abused his position and hid his shame behind the red face and bright tears of a young boy. Now it was over and he was a coward, unmanned by this bullet-hole in his shoulder. Damn… damn.

Still, for all his own weakness what the boy had done was unforgivable. Vellard had turned him twice from a man to a grovelling worm. It would not happen again. He would not allow it. And the boy would know – in no uncertain terms.

Yet even as impotent rage began to make his body quiver the pain from his wound and in his mind grew worse, driving him to gnash his teeth and dig his nails into the palms of his hands in a vain attempt to disperse it. He twisted on his bed, spitting out curses on Vellard and on himself. The universe was saturated with agony, his agony, and it was going to burst his mortal body like a corpse filled with maggots splits before it enters the grave.

But then it had faded to a gentle throbbing. His limbs still thrashed feebly for a few seconds and he heard guttural sounds in his own throat. He subsided into stillness and could hear Madame Delain's breathing, slow and regular on the other side of the ward. He remembered everything again and for a moment his body tensed as it made itself ready for more anguish. But, he realised, it was night. Time for rest and peace. His muscles relaxed, and at the same time the pain in his shoulder subsided to almost nothing. He knew that he could expect uncomfortable dreams, but his body would resist no more. The boy would wait. He closed his eyes in the gloom and slept.

Ricard

Ricard closed the door behind him and leaned against it. Lieutenant Georges' surprised eyes questioned him, but the doctor did not comment audibly. Ricard concentrated on his breathing. It seemed constant, not shuddering too much. This was reassuring, but hardly expected. The whole of France seemed to have slipped into lunacy under his feet. He had only gone to inform Deschaves that Vellard's location had been identified, and he had been confronted with two weeping forms.

The captain was crying quietly. Ricard could see bright tear-tracks running into his mouth. Madame Delain appeared to have been running across the room. Her face was red and screwed up as though in agony. As she ran she had seemed to look at him but of seeing him she gave no sign. He felt offended by that as though she had rudely spurned him. But it was understandable, he reasoned, after all that crawling around in mud. She was badly upset and though he wanted to ease her out of her misery he could not until she had shaken off the worst after-effects of her fever. At any rate, he insisted to himself, dusting imaginary motes off his jacket, what he had had to say could wait. He had to act on it.

This thought troubled him too. As he thanked Lieutenant Georges and suggested to him that he should have a look next door he was aware, vaguely, of speaking in an absent manner. The shift between warmth and cold at the door only struck him when he had walked twenty steps or so. The main part of his mind seemed to have unrolled in front of his eyes so that he could only dimly see where he was going. On the screen that had descended he saw flickering images of the situation he now faced. The soldier who had brought the news to him had crystallised the impending crisis into words.

"We've found Lieutenant Vellard sir. He's got men with him. He fired his revolver at us sir. What do we have to do now, sir, the sergeant says."

The soldier's face had been turned up to his with the jaw thrust forward slightly so that the yellowing front teeth could rest on one another. Ricard remembered how he had considered reprimanding the man for not shaving his hollowed cheeks properly so that he didn't have to answer the question. It was as though he had to undertake the defence of Grenon again under this unfriendly sky and in full view of ranks of those eyes he had seen in Paris.

Of course he had plans, he protested, as though facing the penetrating gaze of Major Desailles again. But they could not be put into action again until… until he knew exactly what it was he was dealing with. More exactly than Vellard's grid reference and the number and names of the men who had not answered the hurried roll call that afternoon – 765910 and 17 respectively – he had to go and look for himself. Then more plans could be made and put into operation. Still, there was one thing he could do for the moment and that was to prevent any danger of him having to act too soon.

"Place pickets. Surround him, but don't shoot unless he tries to escape. I don't want to have to fight a battle."

The soldier had looked relieved. Ricard had dismissed him with a heavy heart. He thought of his plans again. He would have to persuade Vellard – this man who had tried to kill and had wounded one of his officers! This man whose last words to him had been completely lunatic. He would have to persuade Vellard to surrender.

The only alternative *was* to fight a battle. A battle

here, of all places. Now, of all times. More graves. He would be happy to kill Vellard himself – his nails dug into his palms as he made his hands into fists and fantasised about the blood that would pour from Vellard's face. He did not want his men to die in some scrappy skirmish when peace was supposed to be the norm. They would die like Private Dessons not in a war but in a joke, a freak happening. And Lieutenant Vellard professed to care about them…

Ricard paused in thought and stride outside his junior officers' quarters. He realised that his trains of recollection and past thinking had coincided in a condemnation of Vellard. But he had to act, to take on responsibility for whatever would come. He would go and see and act on whatever he saw. If the eyes of Paris would not look charitably on him he would act no differently. He had defended Grenon. He would defend Pericard and Madame Delain.

It was only the knowledge that this was not Grenon that caused him to waver long enough to go into the officers' quarters and find Jannert. The lieutenant was sitting at his table reading *Les Miserables* with rather more interest than the last time Ricard had seen him.

"Sir?"

"Please accompany me, Lieutenant. Lieutenant Vellard has been found. I have given instructions that he should be surrounded. I intend to examine the situation personally, and I would be grateful for your assistance."

"Yes sir. Just one moment sir."

Jannert reached for the stick on which he still leaned. Ricard's heart beat faster, thinking that the lieutenant's stick could help hold off decisions for longer. It would slow the two officers down as they crossed over the battlefield – giving more time, perhaps, for Vellard to surrender. That thought was met by a contrary one, that he

164

should take pity on the older man, especially since he knew how much importance Jannert placed on having "lived through it", and spare him going to the guns again. It also occurred to him that it was better to act quickly. By the time Jannert's sober form was motioning him to go to the door first a sort of compromise had been reached. He, Ricard, would be the one facing the guns. But in that case the longer the trek across the battlefield took the better. If the worst came to the worst it would at least delay the moment of his death.

He almost struck himself with irritation. What kind of melodramatic twaddle was that? He had to be disciplined, and be focused. Dreams of a tragic doom were no use. Men would die equally tragic deaths unless he concentrated. But as the two officers, one upright, the other shambling slowly, made their way through the low buildings towards the wreckage of the open space, Ricard could not truly believe in the reality of what he was doing. Even the physical sensations of his footsteps, heartbeat, the wind and Jannert's hand knocking him slightly as the other man stumbled seemed to be given to him by some other medium than his own senses.

"Are you all right Lieutenant?"

"Yes sir. My leg still hurts a bit though… What will you do, sir?"

"I'm not sure yet Lieutenant. That's why I need your advice."

They moved on in silence. When they reached the barbed wire that separated "the battlefield" from "the village" they stopped and Ricard looked to and fro like a hunting dog that has lost sight of its prey. The single sentry left to guard the difficult path did not offer any information. He picked at his blackened teeth with a sodden match and kept his eyes away from the officers as though to look at them would be to involve himself too deeply in the whole mess. Even as they passed he seemed to salute vague shapes he could see out of the corner of his eye, not them themselves. As they passed him the wind picked up and blew their coats against their thighs. The effort of struggling against the wind almost made the progress over the ground unbearable. Ricard felt his legs beginning to resist him as they drew closer in such conditions to the danger. The slowness of their pace was not improved by Jannert's sudden clarification of what made the whole place seem different.

"Not very quiet is it sir? The wind seems to be so loud I can hardly hear myself think."

Ricard nodded in reply. When he turned his gaze forwards again he saw that the wind was not only noisy. It was making the earth that had seemed dead appear to move, run along with itself, almost flex its scarred features. Where there were plants they followed the wind. Where litter or cloth or other light things had fallen they rolled along as if under their own power.

"I haven't seen it like this before."

Jannert looked at him with very patient eyes.

"No, it has not changed like this for some time sir."

"It is as though Vellard's escape has also changed the weather."

"Perhaps the weather has decided to help you clear up sir."

Ricard frowned. The joke – if it was a joke, though it was hard to see how else to take it if his own comment had been construed as a joke – felt as though there was something sinister in it. If there was, Jannert seemed unaware of it. His eyes did not watch Ricard's response but dropped back to the mud and its contents. Ricard shrugged. He preferred his own interpretation. There were lives to remember. He did not want to have responsibility for the weather as well.

"There, sir."

Ricard followed Jannert's pointing arm. The wind was icy against his eyes but he was certain that what the lieutenant's leather-clad finger indicated was a group of soldiers – three, he thought, lying slumped and still at the bottom of a ridge which was all that was left of a rain-decayed shell crater. He realised that he had been thinking about the scene in the infirmary with Madame Delain but this vision dropped out of his head at the sight.

"Oh no. Not so soon."

"We had better stay out of sight sir."

"Yes, Lieutenant. Have your revolver ready as well."

They went on, bent double, towards the blue shapes on the black mud. It was slow and uncomfortable, but not so slow as trying to crawl through the uneven mess of wire and other metal mixed in with sucking, cloying mud would have been.

Ricard's sense of the danger he and his companion might be in centred on this idea – if they were fired on they would have to crawl and that would be a problem – and on the pain that his position created in a line between his shoulder blades. He was conscious that he had not considered what the sensation of being hit by a bullet would be like, but then he had not thought of that that day on Grenon. On that day instead he had wondered what the anonymous face in the photo frame would have thought of him as he defended his command. She would have been coolly impressed, he remembered deciding. He also remembered that Pericard was not so simple as Grenon had turned out to be and pressed his mind again to the fear he had for the three men. He had not kept a copy of the letter he had sent to the family of Private Dessons, but he did remember the frustration of trying to write it.

He ran the last few yards to the unmoving soldiers, leaving Jannert to get on as he could. They were not dead –

they heard him! They turned, one almost raising a rifle but letting it slip down into the mud. They grinned as he arrived and he transformed the tension that had built up in his chest into a stern, officious demeanour.

"What are you doing?"

"Lieutenant Vellard's been firing at us sir. We took shelter. He's over there to the right sir."

The soldier waved generally over the top of the little ridge. Ricard crawled up beside him, feeling the mud coldly envelop his knees. He inched his way up the bank and peered over as high as he dared. Some more of his own men were visible sitting slumped against other humps of earth, lying smoking in little hollows. One or two of them were doing as he was now doing and watching carefully in the direction that the soldier had indicated. Nothing there could be seen except for mud and wreckage.

"He's in a trench isn't he?"

"Yes sir. There are people watching the trenches on either side. I saw the sergeant send them there. I don't think anything's happened."

"Anyone hurt?"

"Dunno sir. Ask the sergeant. Just over there to the left sir."

"They're not going to shoot at me?"

"I don't think so sir. It's all been quiet for a while."

All three of the men had looked very relieved when they realised it was Ricard and Jannert. They assumed, he supposed, that he knew what to do. So he ran on, every moment expecting to flinch at a gunshot, but only in the end slipping in the mud and feeling the air chill in his throat as he inhaled. He passed from group to group feeling that these men had lived through worse than this. Why shouldn't he? At the edges of his awareness he knew Jannert was faithfully following him, but he gave the lieutenant little thought for the moment. He would need him later.

After five or six minutes he reached the sergeant, who told him where the men were deployed and exactly where, or as near to exact as he could, Vellard was lurking. No casualties, the sergeant said. But men did not want to be here.

"I don't want to be here either Sergeant. Just to the right of that coil of wire? Right."

He could see a dip in the ground and the remains of a line of sandbags. A trench, certainly.

"Well, Lieutenant Vellard never really wanted anything to change. It's probably appropriate that he's chosen to hide there."

"Yes sir."

Ricard turned to the sergeant's sullen face. He thought of the brusqueness with which he had dismissed the men's fears as he moved from group to group. He had also dismissed his own at the time. Though they were veterans who did not want to die a war death after having lived into peace and he was a novice who was unsure of what to do in this suspended battle, their fears overlapped and were mutually comprehensible. At least so he thought. In whatever case, there was no place for them here. It was better to be brusque than – he left the thought unfinished and turned back to contemplate Vellard's refuge.

"You say that there is a ring of patrols just closer to it? Where's the nearest one?"

"Just there sir."

"I don't recommend you go sir. Remember Lieutenant Vellard's already tried to commit murder."

"Thank you, Lieutenant. But as I've said, I don't want to fight him if I don't have to."

"Very well sir."

Ricard knew that he would have to crawl. He eased himself over the ridge lip and began to slither through the thick mud, pulling himself forward on his elbows. This was the situation on which he had concentrated his fears a few moments before and it was as dreadful as he had believed. The ground sucked and pulled at his clothes and things threatened to rip through to his now pale skin. He had visions of being too tired to go on and being lured beneath the surface of the swamp by its apparent softness. Only one hand, the hand that held his gun, would remain when they came to add his body to the pile of those who fell after no-one was supposed to fall.

The inmost patrol had been hidden from him by the unevenness of the ground for most of his journey and he had crawled on in blind faith. But now they were visible at last and he felt his body spilling into the space behind them as though he were a worm pursued out of its tunnel by a chopping spade. The men's surprised faces bore muddy testimony to the fact that they too had struggled on bellies to get to this point. Their eyes were the only parts of their bodies that did not look as though they were formed from the surrounding landscape like macabre children of the trench's foetid air.

Once again he asked and was told where to look. Once again he peered over stones and between little ramparts of ground towards the lair of his opponent. And this time, for the first time in his life it seemed, he saw the head he was seeking. The fingers around his gun tightened convulsively. Vellard too was peering, but with much less circumspection. Ricard saw his young face turn from side to side. He caught fragments of words that ricocheted from the jagged things that struck out from the mud's heavy cloak. Vellard was giving orders, but there was no urgency in what he said, Ricard thought. As he lay there it felt as though the stinking damp would creep up through his chest to infect his whole body before he would see any more. As if in confirmation Vellard remained looking out of his trench. His eyes were still as blue as they had been when Ricard had first arrived in the village but what was visible of his hair under his helmet was matted down to his head.

For a second Ricard looked away from him to the two soldiers who also waited. One of them moved his rifle slightly as though to draw his officer's attention to it. His eyes were distant, alien to Ricard and acknowledging no rapport with him. Ricard looked away from his eyes to the rifle. He shook his head very deliberately. The soldier's eyes focused on him again but otherwise his expression did not change.

Ricard looked back to Vellard and his anger grew again. These men were used to the waiting. Like beasts of burden, they had spent most of the war waiting. Then they spent time waiting where they had fought, piling rubbish onto a waiting cart. Now they were waiting again. They could handle the waiting. If you were waiting you weren't dead. But to be active, to be active here, to be active with guns... that was the war, the part of the war that was death. He, a stranger who had had no war, should not be the one to end the waiting. He knew he might have to still, but still was not yet.

He stared at Vellard with hatred. He knew of course that his line of reasoning about the soldiers still might be entirely spurious – he was not to know what went on in other men's heads. He had merely guessed from Jannert's patient obedience and everyone's quiet, expectant movements, something that he had become aware of again that morning. But his thoughts felt convincing to him. They solidified the gnawing sense of unfairness that had come with the death of Private Dessons and was always threatening to make him kick against the world like a petulant child. While this was processing through his mind he raised a cupped hand to his mouth and prepared to shout.

"Vellard! I know you can hear me. I can see you."

The first chiselling word had made the lieutenant's head spin round. Gratifyingly it had also produced a look of concern on the unwrinkled forehead. Ricard suddenly felt in control of the situation. He wanted to shout again even though he was not sure of what he wanted to say. He wanted to feel the tremor of his voice run through his body on the ground and to make Vellard uncomfortable again. If only he could retain this power he could restore order here again.

"Vellard! You don't need to hide. I won't shoot you. I don't want to fight. Do you? It is the wrong place and the wrong time."

The tremor was the same. The power still felt there within him but it no longer carried. Vellard had not moved. Now he would not answer. He just stared out above Ricard towards the clouds that marked the western horizon.

"Vellard! If you surrender no-one need die. In a war your crimes would not be forgivable. But this is not a war any more."

The lieutenant lowered his gaze. He was looking at where Ricard was lying. He still did not answer. Ricard felt order slipping out from under him. The gaze did not see him specifically but still it defied him, and it defied the wind that changed the battlefield as he argued. Nothing in that face acknowledged either the cold gusts or Ricard's appeal. Then – the revolver, the yellowy spitting and cracking sound that seemed suddenly echoed by a thousand others as though the sound was echoing off every contour in the grey sky.

Ricard had barely had time to move but he had ducked below the miniature parapet of earth as the bullet had shot harmlessly by to spend itself against the air or some battlefield junk. When he looked up again the yellow sparks were coming from over his shoulder. The two men he was with, with unconquered instincts of war, had overcome the phobia of the trigger that they had developed and were firing back. Ricard turned to them with anger that stemmed from his disappointment in them as much as from the fact that his scheme of delay was being disrupted.

"Cease fire! Cease fire! From now on, no-one, I mean *no-one* is to shoot unless I say so or Vellard tries to escape! Pass that message on!"

Order. Even if only temporary, even if only superficial. The noise of the wind whipping by became audible again. The two men looked at Ricard in surprise and then at each other in horror. Their fingers fell from their rifles. Vellard was no longer visible but Ricard did not believe that he was out of earshot. He cupped his hand again.

"Vellard! You can hear me still. I don't want a battle, but I will fight one if I have to. You understand? Either more men can be commemorated – and it will be in my way not yours – or you can surrender and argue before a court-martial – and we'll have to dig no more graves.

"Vellard! You said to me that each man should have his own memory, should be remembered as a whole man, not a name. The only way to do that is to keep them alive. I give you five days. From now. That's… eleven fifty-nine hours on Wednesday. If you have not surrendered by then I will be forced to begin firing again."

The words had taken form as he had spoken, born of his frustration with the lieutenant and with the peculiar contradiction between the words he had spoken when he had been in captivity and his present actions. Now that Ricard had pronounced his ultimatum however there was no movement as though this, the war's last paradox, had itself disappeared to wherever all this mess had been before 1914. Nothing was visible in the trench where the mutineer had been.

Ricard remained staring at the point where he had seen

the lieutenant's head for a few more minutes, somehow expecting something. Something other than the chill of the wind and the earth that seemed to grow greater rather than less the longer he was exposed to it. This was certainly not Grenon. Nor was it the hostile Paris he had been afraid of either. It shouldn't be, he thought, not until Wednesday. He dreaded to think what the moments of waiting might be like then, when the peace of the Armistice would be officially broken again. But there was time before then, time for Vellard to give himself up, see sense and save him, Ricard, from the gauntlet of those eyes. It was not physical danger disguised that he was afraid of, he was sure of that. It would be the men who took the risks, not him. He was afraid of the eyes of the survivors who would have seen and almost suffered the futile deaths that he would have to order.

They had not come yet, he told himself. He turned to the two soldiers beside him.

"You did right to fire. I hadn't told you not to."

He saw one of them cross himself and look in the direction of the shrine and the memorial trench. Ricard followed his gaze and decided that the language of Pericard's own strangeness could give some strength to morale.

"Pray God you won't have to fire again. And when I speak to your sergeant I shall order him to send some men to relieve you."

The soldiers thanked him quietly. Ricard felt ashamed. He avoided their looks and began the long laborious crawl back to where the sergeant and Jannert waited for him with anxious faces.

Ricard was furious as he left the village. He knew that if he glanced over his shoulder he would see Major Desailles still standing by his horse and perhaps talking to one of the sentries. The man was… Ricard did not complete the thought.

He had reported on the crisis surrounding Lieutenant Vellard by field telephone – it was urgent after all – and the Colonel in his quiet room had clearly been brow-beaten by the inquisitive Desailles into sending him in person to investigate. Major Desailles' continual references to "HQ" instead of the poor Colonel certainly indicated that to Ricard.

He had only been told the day before, and all his objections – no accommodation for extra troops, for one – had been brushed aside. This time, grudgingly, he had to acknowledge Blamanchard's perception. Desailles had done exactly what he would have done if he had never come to Pericard. But then he had come to Pericard and what would have seemed right before, what was right for Desailles, was now so alien to everything he had experienced that he almost writhed in fury at the thought of it.

But he had had to give way. Orders were just that, he knew. But Pericard was his area of orders. How could order ever restore itself here if the system of order usurped its own order? Desailles had hardly been in the mood to listen to such arguments. He had not even permitted a greeting to pass his lips as he stepped down from his horse and verbally accosted Ricard.

"How could you let something like *this* happen? It's *exactly* what we were afraid of happening here and it's what we sent you here to *prevent*!"

"With all due respect sir why didn't you tell me this when you sent me here? You sent me here to…"

"I know *very well* why I sent you here. And *don't* be insubordinate, damn it! You should be *apologising*!"

The exchange had gone on much like this for some time. Desailles' arrival had been like the intrusion of a gun battle into a night's sleep for the village. Vellard's mutiny had produced consternation, but also a siege mentality – once again the patience of people who had lost everything. Desailles had produced bustle, but for less momentous reasons. Food, reports, a man to hold his horse and another to stand guard. All these had had to be fetched while in the mean time the smartly-clad major had quietly berated the one who had spent enough time here for the filth of his soldiers to have covered him.

"So you've given him until Wednesday? Two more days' time, eh? Very *honourable*, very *tolerant*."

"He has not threatened anyone except myself sir. There are no prisoners to free. There's nothing to be gained by risking men's lives."

"Your word of honour?"

"I have not given him that. I thought that that would be making the whole situation ridiculous."

"Then you can attack this afternoon. *Don't* contradict me or you'll be going to where *he's* going to end up. *Don't* give the orders yet. I'll do that when *I* see fit. I ought to go and see Captain Deschaves to see if he's got anything to contribute to this whole *sorry* business. Oh yes, I forgot."

Desailles walked along the body of his horse, the reins trailing from a gleaming leather glove, and ran his other hand through the contents of a British Army saddlebag. Ricard recognised the make from his trips to Jamaica. He watched Desailles pull out a package wrapped in canvas.

"Think you *might* be interested in these. Is Madame *Delain* still in the same room as Deschaves?"

"Yes, she's still there. She's still very weak."

"Then I shall ask Lieutenant Georges to wrap her in a blanket in his office for half an hour or so. *You* have half an hour to yourself. I *recommend* you spend it cleaning your revolver. Do not, I repeat, *do not* go near Vellard without me."

"Yes sir."

The major's bright boots skirted round a deep rut as he strode off. Ricard watched him go and then moved away from the village. He would not go near Vellard but he would take a final look at the battlefield before more blood was spilled into the greedy mud.

He had expected the shrine and the communications trench to move him but their stillness, apart from the pathetic fluttering of the paper dedications, simply confirmed the coldness that wrapped itself round his feeling of resentment. He stared at the helmets and rifles for a long time, his mind blank except for angry recollections of what Desailles had said to him. He knew he could not countermand his superior officer. The soldiers' order overrode what right order should be.

When he stood up to leave he was dimly aware that the half-hour Desailles had given him had expired long since. This, for him, settled his mind. No blood would stain his hands. He would only be present under protest. He would give no orders, fire no bullets. He would take the risks that other men had endured for four years and more, and pay his dues at last. And by his hand no woman would be placed in the position of Madame Delain. With the thought of her he felt what he had expected to feel when the memorials in the trench and on the gun battery had actually been visible to him. The muteness of the memories enshrined in that trench seemed to underscore her refrain "for my husband".

At the thought of what drove her the package Desailles had given him came back into his mind. The feeling of its weight falling repeatedly against his thigh suddenly gave it a significance that totally reversed its position in the order of his thoughts. Desailles' words as he had handed it over... the hint of smile on his displeased face... He hurried over the treacherous mud of the battlefield pressing his hand into his pocket and against the rough surface of the canvas.

Celine

The major's entrance had been so silent and furtive that she had barely seen him until he was crouched at her bedside. The expression on his face had changed profoundly. It seemed that at last he had admitted to himself exactly the nature of his interest in her. She felt another surge of affection for him, at that moment only held back by the grip of Jean-Paul's dead fingers. She thought she saw the beginnings of tears in his eyes. When he spoke she could only just hear him above the twisting and turning of Captain Deschaves in his bed. His quiet had been broken by the visit of the new major, Major Desailles. She had been sent outside for its duration with Anne and Marie to talk in hushed whispers. It seemed that the visit of Major Villier concerned these two as well, and the others who still slept in their low hut.

"As I said, the replies for the warrants have arrived – Major Desailles brought them."

In his hand was a sheaf of paper that bore the slight tears of over-eager opening.

"Well? Sir?"

"Read for yourself."

She tried to read his expression. He was straining to look impassive, she could see that. What she couldn't tell was what face lay behind the twitching muscles – whether she had reason to hope or despair. He placed the papers next to her arm and stood up to wander round the long room. He did not go close to her, nor did he approach Captain Deschaves. Instead he just walked slowly. Against the double sound of the captain's discomfort and the major's unease she put out a trembling hand to the papers.

She unfolded them slowly as though expecting misfortune. She was conscious of being at the edge or the end of all her hopes. She could not remember the last time she had been so acutely aware of such things as the crackle of paper and the feel of its quality against her fingers. There were six, no, seven pieces of paper. She did not look at all that was written but let her eyes drop to a black rubber stamp at the bottom right of each leaf. REFUSED *[no attempt must be made to move this body]*.

She flicked through all seven to make sure. All had the same heavy stamp. She felt the small structure of expectation she had built over the previous few weeks disintegrate leaving nothing but a bitter choking in the back of her throat. She knew the others would feel an echo of it through the fog of Lieutenant Vellard's anger and she knew they would guess what she had to tell them.

In a few days they would be deprived of both the bodies and the spirits of their lost men. Celine's first news, brought from the trenches and whispered to Lieutenant Georges, to Anne and to others, had caused weeping and grief. Now this rejection was the failure of all that they had relied upon for consolation in the time to come. And there was nothing else.

She looked up. Major Villier was beside her again.

"They didn't give any reasons?"

"You would have to ask Major Desailles. I believe he was involved in the adjudication."

"May I speak to him, sir?"

"I think it would be difficult. He is planning to flush out Lieutenant Vellard this afternoon."

"Flush him out?"

"Kill, capture, generally eradicate him and the men with him. I think he is afraid that such events will spread, or even that something significant might be reported and create… the wrong impression of Pericard, spread the idea of its peculiarity and its myths."

"He can't."

She said this as a statement of fact, but the major took it as a protest.

"He will. There is nothing I can do. I will be present but unable to act. I will not act. I gave Vellard five days and until then…"

"What about the men?"

"They will do as they are told or they themselves will be shot. I do not think they will fight willingly though so I am afraid for them."

She caught his sleeve. She was devoured by anxiety. The sheaf of warrants slipped to the floor. His attention was entirely hers and she knew she could wield power over him. A few of Lieutenant Deladdier's quiet words in the trenches sounded in her ears again – Lieutenant Vellard must not join them before his time. Major Villier, it seemed to her, had given him his time. She had a duty to her husband regarding Lieutenant Vellard too, even if she could not carry out the one that was most important to him. Jean-Paul had spoken about, had insisted on the lieutenant's "time". She owed him all duties.

"Take me to him."

"Why? I mean – you can't. You're still weak. He is not a man to…"

"I'll speak to him. I think I can save him from having to attack. And I – and the others might gain, perhaps."

She saw the effect that the last two phrases had on him. She could see him working out the implications. She'd promised to avert the impending deaths and to make herself happy. She was brightened a little by the look these realisations brought to his otherwise heavy features. But the eagerness was still tempered with caution.

"I don't advise it. A council of war is hardly the place

for a lady in your delicate state. But I will take you to see Major Desailles. I'm sure he will listen to you – though I don't know whether he will act on what you say. Here – wrap this blanket round yourself. Have you any shoes? Here, here, let me put them on for you."

She stood slowly. She felt the welcome warmth of his hands on her shoulder and elbow through the thick weave of the blanket. Her legs seemed as thin as sticks and they shuddered as though she was being led to her execution. Her weakness and the tension within her combined to daze her as she was led towards the door.

"Wait – the warrants."

"I'll fetch them."

His presence was gone for barely a second and then he was leading her through the door again. Outside it was raining heavily and the wind blew the drops and little rivulets of dark water towards them. Major Villier tried to hurry her without pushing her along too fast, shielding her from the weather with his body.

He guided her in this strangely intimate way to his own hut. All around her she could feel gloom in Pericard, and fear of the new alien major who had taken charge so aggressively. When Major Villier had arrived there had been fear, of course, but also expectation. There were no expectations now, only defeat and more deaths, the sort of feelings that were supposed to end with the Armistice. That, at least, was what she sensed, but the conflicting anguish and exaltation that emanated from Lieutenant Vellard made her struggle to understand it. It was as though the further the war was away, the more confusing it became. In the recent past that had seemed to be going the opposite way – she could try to make sense of her relationship with Jean-Paul – but now…

Now they were at the door of Major Villier's hut, to see another new major. Major Villier had gone inside first.

As she had done the last time she stood expectantly outside the door of a new commanding officer she ran phrases through her head. Again she had something to request that might easily be denied her. Again she had to deal with a man who had little or no understanding of how things really were in Pericard. Her thoughts churned, the rain ran down her face and the middle-aged sentry by the door looked stolidly in front of him after one quick glance. He was a stranger, the new major's man. She almost missed the nervously affectionate presence of Major Villier at her shoulder. But then he was there again, coming out of the door, gesturing for her to go in, and what she though about him was swallowed up by what she was about to say behind the rain-darkened door.

The fingermark sensations left by Major Villier on her arms were by no means the caressing memories Jean-Paul's fingers had left – she could tell that there would be bruises where he had gripped her. But they left a comforting feeling, a feeling of a place that wasn't this one. She was between two opposing rings of rifles, once again slipping barefoot through sucking mud and sharp relics. Even Major Desailles' face was comforting to recall… but she had a duty to perform or attempt. That was what Major Desailles demanded, a "duty".

The men who accompanied Lieutenant Vellard were watching her, she knew, and she was not startled when, as she paused at the brink of the collapsing trench, a hand and face put themselves out from a sopping greatcoat and invited her down. The hand that helped her climb down into the dank space was not gentle but the face was not wholly unfriendly. It grinned rotting teeth through a glistening layer of mud. It coughed in a tired, pathetic way, as though it was a child that had been left to play too long in the street, and to her he was suddenly a man again.

"This way."

He led her only a short distance, but it was enough to show her the difference between the trenches she had known with Jean-Paul and these she hurried through now. Neither were fit for men with any minds at all. But in the other trenches efforts had been made to hide the gruesome reality with gestures towards humanity – there had been duckboards to walk on, little stores of food, men making an effort to keep warm and to pretend that they were not being degraded below even the lice that sucked on them.

Had it not been for the attempts at humanity in Jean-Paul's trenches, she thought, she would have seen the reality like this. Here, there were no such gestures. The bottoms of the trenches were raw mud and the men might as well have been naked – their ribs stuck out through their uniforms. They had the bright eyes and unsteady movements of those who had not slept or eaten for days, and did not expect to. Stagnant puddles in which drowned rats lay marked each bend in the trench, and she almost believed she saw human bones here and there in the debris.

It was the smell that was the worst though. In Jean-Paul's trenches it had been strong but there the men joked about it as though the fact that it came from human flesh was of no importance. Here the smell was older, more experienced and insidious. This was how the war was really fought, but even those who fought in it would have been unable to admit it to themselves. She knew Jean-Paul would not have lived even as long as he did without a feeling that human comforts were within his reach.

But here was a low dugout which belched out foetid air in gusts as though someone was working the lungs of several dead men. The soldier who was guiding her indicated that she should go in. For a second she looked mutely at him, afraid, and knowing her own powerlessness. He only looked back and pointed again. She ducked under the lintel and felt its slime smear along her back. If there had ever been a gas curtain hung there it had long since gone, perhaps rotted or gnawed at by rats. She stood in almost total darkness, only vaguely aware of a figure hardly visible in the gloom. Then he lit a candle.

"Madame Delain, it's not a surprise to see you though I don't know why you've bothered to come to me."

"Can't you tell?"

"I have stopped listening to the people of the village since they began to listen to Villier."

"But even they've decided his view will win, to let the dead be the dead, to let the living..."

"No, no. He is right, but also disgusting, depriving human minds of their space on earth. Well – no matter, I will soon be gone, and so will those around me, and forgotten more completely since we are dead afterwards, after the time. There is an irony there, I suppose."

She did not answer him for a while, struck by the keen self-appreciation he displayed. Physically he was no more than a rat except for the ruined blue of his Army uniform. His lips were drawn back from his teeth, his eyes glittered, apparently without consciousness. But his words were reassured and purposeful, certainly more considered than Major Villier's protests had been when she had proposed her scheme.

"You know that what you want will not be achieved at the hands of Major Villier himself?"

"Another officer has come, has he? Why?"

"I think – Major Villier is beginning – to understand."

"He only understands now? Why have you come to tell me this, do you think it will make a difference?"

"I didn't come to tell you this. Listen, I haven't come either to try and save your life or other lives. I want you to delay. Major Villier gave you a time, and it fits in with what Lieutenant Deladdier told me. You weren't to die before you were supposed to. It's not meant to be a time within your own power. This new major – he'll kill you this afternoon, before the time that was set. For my husband's sake delay. I don't know why they required this, but please delay. Two days. I'm sure it'll be your time then."

Lieutenant Vellard looked around him in the candlelight. It reflected his rat-like movements in the streams of water running down the walls of the dugout.

"They don't know what you're doing do they, they think you're trying to save people, but really you're acting on some vague idea because you think that it will make your husband happy. Very commendable."

He laughed, and it was a genuine laugh.

"You're sacrificing everything for the dead. I approve. But – Noilly! Come in here!"

The soldier shambled in. Celine barely looked at him but gazed intently at Lieutenant Vellard. He made her request seem so pitiful, but to her it was the goal she had lived for since the refusal of the warrant. Major Desailles had contemptuously crushed the papers in his leather gloves as soon as she had presented them to him. Something of her husband's wishes had to be granted and it was going to be this. But Lieutenant Vellard ignored her eyes. He pointed to Noilly.

"This man will not live two more days, if he has a chance to die today, in two days he might die of disease, you will have noticed that the air is not good here. If it can be today it will be today, I think the same, and so do all the others. You only have a whim, we have our only desires."

"No! Why must it be today?"

"We must die in battle, it must be battle, it must be war, or they will not have us. During the war, disease was battle. Private Dessons was an exception, but we must die in battle."

185

"And take other men who don't want to die?"

The question blurted from her lips as part of her sullen resentment that things would not happen as she desired. Everything made no sense, and she was trying to outflank him so she could still win the argument. This would have been Major Villier's argument, she knew, and if she could prove him right she could make herself right.

"It has to be battle."

"Not enough reason!"

She shrieked. She would not be stonewalled. Noilly hurried out into the trench air again. Lieutenant Vellard looked at her with amusement.

"It is enough for you, since it does not concern you. When Villier first arrive you know I wanted the world to stay as it was because I saw no way of going to where I wanted to be, and the battlefield was as close to the goal as was possible, so I loathed him for changing it. I didn't suspect he would be helpful, that he would give me what I desired, and I still loathe him – but I must be thankful to him. It is strange, but soon I will be where nothing is strange to me any more."

"Not even the endings of the trenches in air and in water?"

"No doubt you've learnt that that is irrelevant, and so it is. I don't find it strange."

"Oh but wait! Please don't! My husband's wishes!"

Her rapid switch from bitter calm to desperate pleading took Lieutenant Vellard by surprise. She looked up at him from her kneeling position on the soft floor with tears in her eyes. She herself barely knew how she had come to be there. She had simply challenged his self-assurance, and now she was begging him to condescend to her only wish. Lieutenant Vellard recovered himself first.

"You've failed in your husband's most important desires, your desperation makes that obvious, it's plain enough. After such a failure one more will not make a great deal of difference, so I say no. Nothing you can do will change my mind."

He put out his hand, little more than a dirty claw. She took it numbly and was helped to her feet. No tears welled in her eyes now, because once again there was nothing left. She had dug this hope from despair and now despair had overwhelmed even this chink in its enveloping wall.

As Lieutenant Vellard led her out of his cave and to where men waited to lift her out of the stinking grime she was barely able to lift her head. On the one occasion she managed it she suddenly became envious of the look in Lieutenant Vellard's eyes. He was confident, satisfied and at peace. He lived like something less than a rat, but she could tell that in death he looked for something that would far surpass anything he could have achieved in life. After such a war it was the only route left open to him, as it had been for Jean-Paul, she supposed. He had not dared to go home in life, but he wished to in death. At this her thoughts came full circle back again to her failure and her shoulders slumped a little more.

A few more seconds passed in scrabbling and crawling, and she was on her feet in the full force of the rain again. She made her way back along the rain-washed footprints she had left on her outward journey. She felt herself moving slowly, but at last she was within sight of the two majors and Lieutenant Jannert. The rain had soaked through to their skins and their teeth chattered with a cold she barely felt. Major Villier offered her his coat, but she made a slight movement to decline it. He made her press her body into the mud next to him. She did not resist; she did not care. Around her there was activity – men crawling to and fro, Major Desailles leaping upright to shout to Lieutenant Vellard, and then the sound of a single gunshot and Major Desailles crouching again behind the mound of sandbag remnants while Lieutenant Vellard's voice darted its way between the raindrops.

"We have received and returned your messenger, we will accept no terms. We will not surrender, we shall be making an attempt to cross into Germany very soon. If you try to stop us, we will resist."

This public confirmation of her failure brought Celine back into immediate contact with her surroundings. She could see Major Villier's face screwed up against the rain and frowning even more deeply. Lieutenant Jannert was shaking his head, while Major Desailles seemed to be thinking of a reply. She looked out towards Lieutenant Vellard's trench but the rain ran into her eyes and stung them. It seemed to form a shimmering mist between her and the trench so that they were obscured from one another. She narrowed her field of vision to the mud in front of her, which was being constantly reshaped by the heavy drops. As she did so she became more fully aware of what was happening next to her. The tension between Major Desailles and Major Villier had not cooled after Lieutenant Vellard's reply. Instead the argument ran in the same manner as it had before.

"I told you it would not work – you risked her life... now you risk the lives of these men – an act of complete irresponsibility!"

"It is *just* as irresponsible to give any leeway to men and ideas like *these* – I gave you and him a last chance by sending her. Now the *consequences* will follow."

"You're so dispassionate! They 'will follow'!"

"*Yes*, they *will*. Are you with me, or *not*? Lieutenant Jannert, *you* are injured. Will you escort Madame Delain back to the village?"

"Am I? What are you implying sir?"

Lieutenant Jannert did not begin an argument of his own. He did not look very happy about his task, but it seemed that he would accept it. Celine envied him, too. He certainly would be going home to Verdun. He would succeed in his goal. Major Villier was not so submissive.

"I will remain here sir. But I will not be responsible for what follows. I will not act except to protect my men."

"Inactivity is to promote *mutiny*! By *God* – Major Villier, I *formally* relieve you of your command and *require* you to return to the village. I *won't* arrest you, yet, not unless you resist further."

In that moment the fight seemed to go out of Major Villier. As Celine had in the face of Lieutenant Vellard's intransigence, he slumped, and his head fell forward. She knew that his distress must be less than hers, but she appreciated how profoundly he was hurt by the disgrace.

"Yes sir."

"Well *go* then, *damn* you!"

Major Villier did not answer, but threw himself forward against the ground and began to crawl as though he had crawled for years up to this point. Major Desailles looked at his back with a stony gaze. Between the two of them Celine watched and waited for Lieutenant Jannert to begin to lead her back.

In the village, back on their feet, the three of them wandered dispiritedly between the low huts. Celine felt the misery of the people behind the wooden walls on such a day gather round her, almost between her skin and the rain. At her side, Major Villier and Lieutenant Jannert talked in low voices as the water that plastered her hair to her face began to rinse the battlefield's filth from their uniforms.

"I'm sorry for you sir."

"Thank you, Lieutenant. He treated you the same though. Sent you back here."

"I know, sir, but he was right. Look at me, I can barely walk still. He gave me the chance of going back home to

Verdun. Anyway, I was wrong to try and make the Army important to me after the war. I'll resign my commission tomorrow and go home. My job will be finished by then whatever the Army thinks, I'm sure, and I'll be free to leave."

He looked at Celine as he said this, acknowledging the role her news had played in his decision. In the meantime Major Villier looked at him sadly. Then he too looked across at her. She suspected that he guessed what was going through her mind as she listened to Jannert.

"Madame Delain? Will you go home too?"

She pitied his broken tone. Like her, he was on the verge of losing everything he had thought was of value to him. But he could not grant Jean-Paul's wishes and she could not try any more.

"I'll go. Not home, though. I'll go to Paris, and see what I find."

It was a lie, but an innocent one. At least, the false aspect of it, Paris, could not hurt him more than the true. He nodded. There was a long pause. In that pause Pericard was again disturbed by the sounds of war. Gunfire and shouts or screams. Celine felt her back stiffen as she heard them. The faces of the two men were impassive, but she saw them look at each other. Major Villier spoke again. He tried to speak loudly to hide the noises of battle, but his voice quavered too much for it to be effective.

"Well, at any rate, we should get ourselves warm. There's no point in dying from the cold."

A little gesture towards a smile found its way on to his lips, but then was gone again, as though washed away by the water that ran through his hair. Lieutenant Jannert nodded slowly in agreement.

"I shall escort Madame Delain back to her quarters sir. Then I'll go to mine. I shall see you tomorrow sir. I won't resign until all the tasks that come up tomorrow have been completed."

"I know."

Celine admired the formality of his farewell. It was a salve to all their prides, she recognised, and a statement of loyalty. The patient man had offered all he could to his officer. She wondered if Major Villier had understood, for he simply nodded and left them without saying any more. But then she could not sense what he felt beyond seeing what he did. Lieutenant Jannert offered no further comment either once the major had gone, but simply led her to the comparative warmth and dryness of her hut where Anne and Marie waited quietly in the semi-darkness to comfort her and bring her close to the fire. When Lieutenant Jannert's halting steps had stopped banging on the boards of the floor and he had gone out into the rain again, Celine threw herself back on her bed and put her hands over her eyes. A cloud of darkness swept over her that weighed on her more heavily than sleep.

The train was pulling out, swathed in steam and smoke, smelling of oil and the dryness of summer dust. She ran alongside it for a few steps, keeping up with his carriage. As the train picked up speed and pulled away from her he finally made it through the bodies blocking his way to the window and put his head out into the warm coastal sunshine. At the sight of him she could no longer run. He smiled at her as he was carried away, but she could see behind the smile. She could see the terror that he might never come back to her. All the confidence she had been able to build around his assurances shattered and the arm she had lifted to wave farewell fell heavily to her side. She choked and her head turned from the dust and the aching sight. The sound of the train began to diminish. She pressed her lips to keep the feeling of his last kiss in them but her tears seemed to wash it away. It was lost, like him.

At last she was able to look again, and see the rearmost carriage of the train seem to stop as it approached a bend. Her heart leaped – she almost believed that the whole train had stopped, that he would be brought back to her, even if only for an hour, half an hour, a minute... But the pause was only momentary and all the words that she meant to say, that she loved him over and over again and she was sorry, so sorry that she had dared fritter away their time together caught in her throat as they subsided to remain unsaid. Her only comfort was to repeat the mantra with which he had kept both of them sane over these last two aching days.

"I am coming back, I will come back. Look what I have to come back to..."

Into this cloud the voice of Major Villier fell and seemed to spiral between unreal images.

"Madame Delain...? Celine? Madame Delain?"

She opened her eyes again. He was crouched over her as he had been when she had surreptitiously observed him in the infirmary. As he had then, he shrank back at her response, letting what he had had in his hand drop noisily to the floor. The look of surprise on his face turned into a grin of triumph. Behind his she could see the taut faces of the other women. Yet from them she could feel something positive, something growing that made her turn her eyes back to the major's still wet features. He had grown a lot older, it seemed to her, since she had first seen him. He reached into a pocket and drew out the pieces of paper that had caused her such pain. The refused warrants were still crumpled in the same way, just as when Major Desailles' fist had closed over them. He put them on the bed. She pushed them away from her, still not knowing what he wanted, but remaining expectant from feeling what the other women felt.

"Why have you brought these again?"

"Because they don't matter."

"What?"

That grin still played around his face. She dared not guess at his meaning, not after so many defeats.

"Major Desailles has still not beaten Vellard. If we hurry, those warrants will not matter. You can take your husband home."

She sat up and knocked the crumpled warrants to the floor. She gasped for words, but they only emerged as stammering and confusion.

"Quickly – dress and come outside. I will wait there. But hurry – I can't tell when Major Desailles will come back."

He bent to pick up the thing he had dropped. It was his revolver. At the sight of it a bolt of fear went through her, replaced immediately by exhilaration. She saw it as a sign of determination, of a power that would help her overcome all that impeded her.

"Hurry!"

He said this over his shoulder, his face framed by his cap and his hair. It was easy to see that he was as eager as she to get under way. The door slammed behind him. Celine began to pull on warm clothes – it had been night through the open doorway – and the other women gathered round her, clamouring about what the major had said. But Celine wanted to ask no questions. She felt that something had triggered him into action at last and he would act as though he had nothing to lose. She could almost have loved him for that.

She breathed in fume-filled, sweaty air as though it were nectar. And the one phrase ran round and round her head in which she believed as though Jean-Paul himself had spoken it. "You can take your husband home."

Within two minutes she was as dressed as she was

prepared to be. It seemed to her that she did not cross the wooden floor of the hut but was instantly in the chilly air seeing her breath rise up in clouds between her and the figure of the trembling, exultant Major Villier.

Ricard

He kept looking at the gun in his hand. The dull metal was now sparkled with rainwater that reflected the light of the lamps that had been brought out to assist the work. He had his back to the light, looking out into the dark where the battle between Desailles and Vellard had died down to occasional gunshots and shouts. There had been no soldiers returning from the battlefield as yet but this did not reassure him. Every moment he expected Desailles to come tramping back into the village leading his – not his – bloodstained soldiers and a pile of bodies and moaning wounded.

Unless all the work was done by then they would be foiled again and he would be less than nothing. He looked at the gun again, as though weighing up the potential it offered. He let it fall to his side. Though he was not watching it, he could hear how fast the work was going. It was not fast enough. The cart was waiting with the man at the horse's head, but every second before it started to move was a second in which Desailles could come back.

The revolver. He had never aimed it so close to a man that he could register what the bullet did to him. But then again, he had never been so sure in his life that were he forced to aim this one time he would also be capable of pulling the trigger. He *would*. Desailles had enough blood on his hands, and for Ricard any blood spilt now would only add to Desailles' guilt. Desailles had decided to fight again; Desailles would face the consequences.

The certainty of this belief had come with the germination of the plan that he was now executing. In his quarters, in the dark, he had practically ground his teeth in futile resistance to Desailles' actions and to his own dishonour. With Desailles' arrival everything that he had done in Pericard was negated. Even his own identity had been denied him: "You are relieved of your command." Here had been promotion, responsibility, the first step on the road to success in a career he had never expected would so reward him. And now – "You are relieved of your command."

In that phrase he was rejected by what he had believed would support him throughout his life. The Army refused him; he turned to the only other source of support he could find. In that he would succeed, outside the Army. Within it he had had failure forced upon him. He had only realised the extent to which he needed her, his support, in the last few hours, in the time since he had seen that crude stamp-mark on each of the women's applications.

In that moment, when the tears had forced themselves out unexpectedly, he had known what Madame Delain meant to him. What exactly it was, he was not sure. He was fascinated by her determination, that was true, and perhaps if she were not so filthy she would be attractive to see, but… He wondered if it was simply the fact that she had been willing, even if only in a confused way, to speak to him as though he mattered to her. That was a feeling that he was not used to, as the anonymous picture in the frame testified. Celine – he shivered as he allowed himself the use of the name – would not simply have been 2coolly impressed" by any success he may have had, he was sure. Whatever the direct source of his feelings, the two of them were inextricably linked now. She too had been refused by the Army. Together they would reject its power over them.

This had been his thought in the heat of the moment. In the sobering rain in which he now stood he had abandoned ideas of togetherness. He was doing it for her, that remained true, but she was still doing what she did for her husband. Nonetheless, their goals were the same. But so would their defeat be if Desailles caught them.

He moved further out of the circle of lamplight so that he could see towards the battlefield more clearly. Every instinct in him urged him to turn round and to throw his weight in with the men from the village, and the women – those who were not too old or ill – who were digging.

Their voices rattled in their throats with the effort as they gasped and struggled. He had persuaded himself that he heard Madame Delain's breathing distinct from that of the others. She had taken up a spade in spite of his protests about her weak condition. The effort she put in only served to underline his conclusions about her motives.

He, on the other hand, stood aside from the digging like Anne Lamarque, whose fingers ran in and out of the grasp of the others as she stood under her shawl at the graveside. They were at Private Lamarque's grave now and as they had broken the ground with their spades he had heard her thin voice quavering prayers that had seemed to carry further even than the sounds of picks and exclamations across the treeless landscape.

Ricard had been appointed, or had appointed himself, to defend the knot of struggling limbs. The immediate threat was minimal – there were few soldiers left in Pericard, and Ricard had taken care to ensure that none of them knew what was happening. None therefore could betray him; none therefore could be held responsible for what was happening. It was the less immediate threat, Major Desailles' threat, for which they had to be prepared and which, if truth be told, would rather require cunning and delays than the sharp violence of the pistol, that he watched for.

Behind him there was a collective sigh. He risked a glance in that direction and saw that the coffin, its walls already weakened by damp and by the mouths of crawling things, had at last been brought to the surface. Like the others before it, it stank. The diggers shrank away from it for a second, and quickly covered it with cotton sheets that, if they did not confine the smell, at least prevented the coffin's contents from being visible through the gaps in the wood.

Ricard looked away from the scene as soon as the busy motions of lifting and dragging the coffin to the cart, which stood on the other side of the cemetery next to the road, had begun. Even as those noises reached his ears he could hear the gasps that accompanied metal breaking into the soft earth again at the next grave. Ricard had to restrain himself from crying out to them to work faster. It would hardly be fair, and indeed it might be enough for the less enthusiastic men to throw down their tools altogether. The priest of the village had, surprisingly, Ricard thought, given his blessing to the enterprise, a blessing sweetened with offers of Ricard's own money, and most of the men had eagerly pushed themselves forward, but even so, he suspected that there would be not unnatural doubts about what was taking place. So he subdued his voice and only muttered to himself what he wanted them to hear.

"Come on, come on! He's going to be back! Come on! We haven't got all night!"

Then, with a realisation so icily clear that he even shivered with the awareness of it, he saw a flare go up on the battlefield. Its brightness made even the diggers stop and turn. He heard their voices as the landscape was touched by the lurid pink glow. Every contour of the ground, every knot in the wood of the village seemed to be glowing with the intensity of it.

Ricard's heart lurched as much for the men who must necessarily be dead at that moment as for the implications for himself of that signal. It could only mean that the combat had ended. Desailles had won, as he must, and he

198

had sent the flare up into the night sky to summon the survivors, if any, back into his control. The immediate concern though was that they had to work faster. The sounds of effort had not started again and he turned round to them fixing his face as sternly as possible.

"Keep going! There is no time to stop trying now!"

They were a mass of lit forms to him, some unnaturally shortened by their depth in the ground, others still in the posture of work, frozen in fear by the alien light that had come upon them and now faded, leaving them more isolated than before in their pool of lamplight.

"Hurry!"

This last word, intended by him, but spoken by the unmistakable voice of Madame Delain at last prodded them into action. They moved again and he heard the bite of cold metal in the ground once more. He turned back towards what he had to observe. His face felt colder now, as though the lamplight gave off heat that no longer reached him. He felt his fingers tight on the revolver and he concentrated his mind on looking for any signs of activity. But there were none.

He had no idea how long he stood there in a state of continuous alert. Long enough for Private Lamarque's coffin to have been loaded into the patient cart and for that team to have returned. He heard the anxious questions and the flurry of sounds as tools were taken up and lamps moved to the last of the graves. This final site was some way from where he stood, and in the diminished light he began to see the shapes of the village in the middle distance more clearly. Desailles would go there first. He had to, for he had no reason to suspect that anything was happening out here amongst the war dead. He would have his own dead to deal with in any case.

Then there! He had been right! There was light in the village, a single spot of it that swung from side to side, like incense in a church, he recalled from his childhood.

"Cover your lamps! But do as much as you can! I'll try and delay them. Somehow – tell me when you have finished. If you can't, make sure he doesn't see you!"

He hissed these words at the graveside without warning. The diggers had barely a moment to glance up at him, and then he was running between the graves, his coat blowing open and catching around the barrel of his revolver.

He would be in the village in two, three... five minutes. He quickened his pace, always on the verge of losing his balance as the mud caught at his battered boots and falling against the hard edges of a grave marker. At last, the village, but he was stained with sweat, it ran down into his eyes and his breath came long and shudderingly as though he was on the verge of tears. He tried to calm it as he rested for a moment against the safely solid wood of one of the huts.

His hand came away dripping from his face. He rubbed his skin with a scruffy jacket cuff and breathed deeper, slower breaths. The revolver was too heavy, his wrist shook to hold it; he could not look innocent if he held it anyway. Hurriedly, he put it away, and at once felt more relaxed, as though the tension of the situation was partly buoyed up by the gun.

And yet, in spite of all this he still could not move naturally, only jerkily, on the edge of collapsing like broken puppet. A clear thought came to him and he scrabbled in his pocket for his cigarettes. He held one in twitchy fingers for a few seconds. Then he lit it and pushed himself off the wall and round the corner and into the main street of the village.

As it came into view the cigarette almost dropped from his fingers as the calm he had so elaborately put on evaporated. Men were lying across the whole space, some moving, some still. There were groans and cries for help and at the edge of hearing, the priest's words murmured low and reverentially. On some of them Ricard could see the blood spreading over their clothes even as he watched. Some were on stretchers, others simply lying on the wet ground clutching at their legs, their arms and their bellies. He ran closer, unable to take it in, and he saw their faces. There was one, twisted with pain, another in a fixed stare, his lips moving silently.

He knelt by this one but the man didn't seem to notice him. He was wrapped up in a world of agony and the battlefield was drying on his face, a mask over the mask of his features. Ricard stood, suddenly aware that he still held the cigarette in his hand. He threw it to the floor and stamped on it in a rage, beginning to look wildly around for the perpetrator of the carnage, to find him and impale his throat on some dead man's bayonet.

"Major Villier?"

He turned, half raising a fist as he did so. It was Lieutenants Georges and Jannert with a group of about ten men. The two officers were stony-faced but the men behind openly showed their grief at the sudden appearance of this massacre in lives that had thought such things to be at an end. Some were even sobbing.

"It is over then?"

"Yes. The usual casualty rate. Nothing's really changed sir."

Lieutenant Georges' voice was long-suffering. With a visible effort he turned to the men behind him and ordered them to start tending to those who were still alive, bind their wounds and take them in out of the rain.

"How many like this?"

"I don't know sir. I know that most of the others are dead. About the same number on each side. And on… ours, many more wounded. There will be a roll call tomorrow sir. If you'll excuse me, sir."

"Go on."

Lieutenant Georges crouched next to the nearest man and reached into the heavy bag he was carrying. Ricard suspected that he had a long night ahead of him.

"More graves to dig, sir. We have to know their names first though."

Lieutenant Jannert put his hands up to his face like a man feeling his age for the first time. Ricard was about to answer but he was interrupted by a bawl, a commanding bellow from the direction of his own quarters.

"*Villier*! Come here! *Immediately*!"

Ricard looked with wide eyes at the dead and wounded. He looked into Jannert's tired and patient face and realised that both of them had loathed the long waiting. Now it was over, they almost wished for it to start again. The he remembered the cemetery and his plan afoot there. He looked again at Jannert.

"Good luck, sir."

"Thank you. Have a good journey home."

Ricard felt cold run through his shoulders but pushed himself towards fatalism. Whatever happened now, he hadn't far to fall. Men had died in spite of him, but with any luck he would give Celine and the others a semblance of their happiness back. With that thought in mind he squared his shoulders and lifted his head out from the quagmire of despair into which he felt it had fallen, and made his way to his old quarters. On the way he remembered the ploy he had had in his mind before he had seen the lolling heads in the mud of Pericard's street. He presented himself to the sentry outside with a cigarette in his hand and, he hoped, a certain confidence in his step. The sentry stood aside for him and he went in suppressing his fruitless anger and trying to concentrate on buying time for Celine and the other diggers.

"Where have you been, Villier?"

He showed the cigarette to him as a defence. Desailles was grim-faced, still smeared with the grime of his battle. His voice was quieter and there was none of the triumphalism Ricard had expected in him, only a certain determination in his movements as though, more definitely than before, he would overcome many things in order to get what he desired. One of the reasons Colonel Blamanchard had said they were alike was that neither of them had fought in this war. Ricard suddenly felt a flicker of pity for the man. He had had no real idea of what he was going to become involved in. It was a situation, as he well knew, in which training counted for nothing without true comprehension.

"Have you been successful, sir?"

"Yes. Put that damned cigarette out."

Desailles was sitting at the desk, tapping his pen on his teeth as he had done when Ricard had met him in his own office. With his free hand he ran his thumb across the bound pages of Ricard's journal of his life on Grenon. Not invading, simply making another sound. When he spoke, he spoke deliberately as though unwilling to waste any more of his allotted time span arguing with fools.

"I would charge you, Villier, with *wilful* negligence, but, after tonight, I shall be on some level merciful. In any case, I need you for the trial. You will, of course, leave…"

"Trial, sir?"

"Oh yes. I mean to make an example of Lieutenant Vellard and – what's his name? – Private Noilly."

"They're alive sir?"

Ricard ran his hand down his face. All those men dead and not Vellard?

"Yes. *Yes*."

Desailles suddenly leaned forward and placed his

grimy hand over his face.

"As I was saying, *don't* interrupt me, you will not remain here, but take a desk job in Paris. If you co-operate in the trial, that is where you will stay."

"Yes sir."

"Oh yes, I need you to confirm the identity of Private Noilly. He's in the infirmary. I will take you there myself."

Ricard stood, totally bewildered. Somehow the evening's events had been wrenched from his control, but the man responsible for that wrench himself seemed unable to control events. As Desailles stood he could see the aches and the effort to concentrate that wracked him. Major Desailles had not been left unmoved by what he had done – yet he had killed those men! Ricard tried not to think further about this. This expedition to see the captured men seemed to be exactly the kind of diversion he had been hoping for. This, for certain, would give Celine enough time to get the bodies safely to the cart, and a little away.

This had been his goal; he was certain he had succeeded. But now he had more things to consider. As he walked back with Desailles from the infirmary, each of them carefully making no reference to the lines of dead and wounded that lay beneath sheets and the weary ministrations of Lieutenant Georges and his volunteers, he reflected on the sudden change in Lieutenant Vellard.

Ricard had been sure the man was mad when he last interviewed him before his escape, but at least he had seemed alive. Now, he was still alive, albeit wounded three times, but the humanness in him was gone. No thoughts, not the faintest flicker of spirit seemed to trouble his catatonic features. Noilly was the same. It was as though, not being dead, the two of them simply opposed life. Having seen the faces and heard the cries of those who had been compelled to leave their lives, Ricard was infuriated by what appeared to be their last arrogance. Even Desailles seemed to be shocked by the depths to which his prisoners had sunk.

There could be few people whom Vellard detested more than Ricard, yet when he had entered the room and spoken in low tones to Desailles formally identifying the other lumpen form in the corner as Noilly, Vellard's eyes had not registered him at all. The only sign that he was not actually dead that Ricard saw was a slow shifting of gaze from the wall to Noilly when his name was pronounced. Ricard did consider attempting to explain the condition rationally but there seemed to be little point. No-one could say for certain what had happened in Vellard's mind in the last few days, particularly not when Desailles had reintroduced gunfire to the trenches… But this brought his mind back to Desailles' eagerness for killing. He had to know the sad little skirmish in the grime would produce consequences.

"What will happen to them now sir?"

"Who?"

"Lieutenant Vellard and Private Noilly sir."

"They'll be court-martialled. I *suppose* that the defence will plead insanity and get them put away somewhere, but that's not the point. The point is that other officers will be able to benefit from our work here at Pericard and to nip signs of this 'war trauma' or whatever the defence will call it, in the bud."

"For the good of the Army then?"

"Oh yes. To whom else does it pertain?"

Ricard made no comment. They progressed a little further down the street in the dingy light of the lamp hung outside the infirmary. Then there were running steps behind them. Ricard's heart began to thunder against his ribs. What was this? Some disaster at the cemetery?

"Don't be so jumpy Villier. It's just the casualty

figures I requested from Lieutenant Georges. Thank you, soldier."

The man who had splashed the forty or fifty metres through the mud to reach them saluted and turned his back on them to walk slowly back to the infirmary. Desailles opened the neatly folded piece of paper and looked for a minute or two at what was written on it. When he folded it back up his demeanour had changed. It seemed that while he was considering the capture of Vellard he was able to inject a note of dry amusement into his comments. Now, on the other hand, he was simply businesslike. He did not offer to show the paper to Ricard. They began to walk side by side again to Desailles' quarters.

In the meantime Ricard's mind had turned fully again to Celine and the cemetery. He hoped desperately that they had got away, but at the same time a desire moved within him to see Celine again, even if only for a second, before she went. Now he found the flaw in his plan which was otherwise so practical and effective. He was allowing Celine to go – sending her away in fact. He felt he could stand that. But to be up to his neck in dead men and legal formalities while she went... he curled his toes inside the hard leather of his boots in an attempt to direct the frustration of his body there and away from any visible signs he might show. He thought about the last moment he had seen her, her mouth half-open between physical effort and surprise, bent over, her spade in her thin hands. Her head had been turned to him as he spoke so that the light from the lamp shone directly into her face and hid the dirt on her skin that degraded her. She had not spoken to him – the last word he had heard her say was directed to the other diggers –

"*Villier*! Listen when I ask you a question! Who is that *man* over there? Is he signalling to us? Draw your revolver. I'm suspicious. *Quick*, let's follow him."

Ricard emerged from his regretful musings with a jolt of realisation of his own stupidity. What else had he said as he had hurried off? What else…? "Somehow – tell me when you have finished." And of course that was what they were doing. They had not had a chance before because of the business with Vellard, and they were doing what they had been told. Only he, Ricard, had been thinking about them – her – too much and so failed to notice his own signal. Until Desailles, the worst person possible to even see it, had pointed it out to him. And now Desailles was running, heavy-footed, after the little man, who, suddenly confronted, was sprinting as fast as he could towards the place he felt safest, which was, as Ricard realised with a sinking heart, the cemetery. Desailles would find out. Desailles would stop them!

Swallowing in a suddenly parched throat, Ricard began to run, almost experimentally, as though he was unsure of his control over his quivering limbs. It was downhill to the cemetery and as he picked up speed, running blind through the whole field, he lost any ability to restrain his pace and he rushed through the dark, hoping his foot would not catch on anything, hoping that Desailles would fall, and give the messenger a chance.

The ground levelled as he reached the cemetery and after a few long, ungraceful strides he managed to curb his speed and to look around him and listen, though it was a cloudy night and nothing really moved in the blackness under the cloud layer. Then – two reports, two flashes of light that barely illuminated the hand of the gunman. Ricard waited for any further sound, a cry, an answering shot, anything that might give him a clue about where people were and what they were doing. Out of the corner of his eye he saw lights come on here and there in the village but he turned his back on them. They could not help him. He had to penetrate the darkness in the opposite

207

direction. Shuddering breaths stabbed sudden pains through his ribs. He could feel the softness of mud under his boots; he was sure he could feel his eyes growing larger in his head like an owl's as he tried to see into the gloom.

The shots were not repeated. After a few minutes a point of light, orange and not fixed to a single spot but moving backwards and forwards, appeared somewhere towards the other side of the cemetery. Nervously, unsure what to expect if he got there, Ricard began to move towards it. Back he went through the cemetery, not skittering around the graves, terrified to touch them as he had been earlier, but slowly, resting his hands on the horizontals of the cold crosses, watching to see what the light would do next. It still moved back and forth and as he drew closer to it. It became clear to him that someone held the lamp and was striding to and fro. But still no sound had followed on from the revolver shots, except for the quiet, furtive ones made by Ricard himself.

At last he had reached the cemetery's edge and there were no more graves. The light was close now, so close that Ricard was beginning to see the shapes of the people around it. Anxiety drained away from him and was replaced by the sense of defeat he had become familiar with. By the time he stepped into the circle of lamplight, seen by and able clearly to see whom it surrounded, he already knew what he would find. A line of terrified villagers, Celine and the other women, and Desailles, revolver in hand, glaring at them as he stalked from one end of the line to the other.

Vellard

He had known these faces since he had been a boy, and he knew them well, knew them in these expressions, these mocking grins and hostile eyes. He knew the laughter too, coarse and grating like beasts. They knew that they could always make him weep, and it was not too hard for them to make his cheeks as red as his lips and the tears come coursing down his cheeks onto his chest. They pushed against him, knocking him to the ground and he felt rough stones under him, his hands pushing up against other hands and watery sun on his face. They laughed louder and prodded him with their toes and he knew that here, behind the old brick schoolhouse they could do what they wanted with him. He lashed out feebly and lost a shoe and they laughed even more ferociously and he had to limp home. But now he was a man. They could not do this any longer.

And it really seemed that they could not. Their faces were retreating and dull fear was in their eyes. They no longer laughed openly though one or two still smirked behind their hands. A strong hand, used to the confidence he craved too abjectly ever to attain, took him by the shoulder and he was on his feet in the sunlight, or was it lying placidly in a copse of trees and he was a man at last able to face the worst his life could throw at him.

But the touch of the hand had grown rough of late, and he began to regard it with fear, no longer with the gratitude and affection he had become used to. But, too, he was a creature of habit that dared not turn against the hand in case it took away the strength he had found in himself, or been granted, until the day it took him as a sacrifice, offered him up to those laughing evil faces that had so often beaten him to the ground. He shuddered and tried to turn his strength against the strength that had so betrayed him, but he was brushed aside and fell ignominiously at their mercy.

But they had changed, changed into what he was not sure, but the smiles were friendly not hostile, and the blow that had fallen to crush his skull had become a tender caress... he knew that touch... Vincent – his brothers. They were consoling him, ruffling his hair as they had always done to the family's youngest, and he relaxed at last, comfortable in this ring of familiar affection. Yet not so familiar, for their faces were sallow and there was something more wrong with them, something he could not identify unless, unless... Lord God! They were decaying. He reached out for Vincent's face. It was swollen and the flesh was spongy to the touch. He pulled his hand back in horror. His brothers were dead, dying before him, dying beneath a glowering sky and high walls of mud out of which hung wire and rotten cloth. Now there were thousands of them clustering round him, towards him, and hands were reaching out to claw him. He recognised the faces, disintegrating as they were... his men and friends all staring at him. He dared look no longer at his brothers. They were calling him, demanding that he join them. Forward, forward his mind insisted. They were his family, his comrades.

Despite the horror he must accede. He must join them. But his body would not act though he willed it forwards with every fibre of his soul. No! It went back with animal revulsion, ignoring his fighting, and even the tears which flowed of their own accord. Back, back he went, reeling away from them, choking on his nausea. They followed but could not close the distance.

His body fell against something solid. At last he could

retreat no further. They would reach him soon, but... They had stopped, and looked up and over him with an emotion akin to fear. He twisted his head and his fear followed theirs. Henri was there, blocking his path with his arms folded despite the blood which seeped from his shoulder. Behind him was another form, more massive but without the hostility that oozed from Henri. It was Major Villier.

Henri's eyes were filled with the pain of betrayal, and... he shuddered. Hate. Hate that would keep him alive when he desired death above all else. He felt Henri's hands seize him. Not the gentle hands he had felt at first, nor even the rougher ones that had followed them, but worse, worse, hands that promised torment without release, hands that promised to bring him back to life and aeons of lonely life when he should have gone forward to his death and joined the welcoming embraces of his dead, decaying comrades. He writhed in the grip of life until another touch startled him into hope. This touch – he knew it too though not so well as the others. Another face appeared before him and he recognised it, and he felt himself smile. Private Noilly!

It was a dirty face and the fingers that gripped him seemed too weak to contest against the intensity of Henri's grip. But then, unexpectedly, there was room to hope more. On the edge of his perception he saw Major Villier's massive form begin to move slowly, excruciatingly slowly until his huge open hand was open towards Henri. It reached and reached and at last the fingers brushed against Henri's arm.

Henri turned in obedience to the touch, and suddenly the grip relaxed. He fell into Private Noilly's arms. He was free. He looked towards the circle of the dead and saw another shape risen above them, shining, the source of its own glorious light. It was as though the Living God had risen to take him, to justify all his faith and to end all his pain. The light grew and by it he could see his comrades opening their arms, beckoning him into their embrace.

He stumbled forwards a couple of steps and stopped. Why? Why had he stopped? He looked behind him. Henri and Major Villier still stood there, but motionless, gazing on him with fixed eyes. They had not stopped him. Yet he could go no further forwards. He looked for Noilly but found there no comprehension, only terror. The dead were still beckoning but he could not go to them. The form in the light put its fingers to its lips. Then he understood.

They must wait. Soon the last call would summon them and they would be able to go to their destiny. Until then they must wait, wait between the living and the dead in the gentle light of the God to whom they were going.

Celine

When he appeared out of the darkness she felt safer. No-one could tell how long he had been standing there because their eyes were so firmly attached to Major Desailles, but as soon as her eyes had found him others followed. Each moment of recognition was occupied by a redefinition of what they all felt.

The tension that had combined in them had remained the same since Major Desailles had fired two shots in the air just behind the cart and caused them all to turn and a lamp to drop from the hand of Jacques. The flame had flared and faded, alternately showing their frozen postures and hiding their frightened faces.

Major Desailles had not immediately said anything. Still with his revolver in his hand, he had bent and stood up the lamp. He had knelt beside it and restored the flame to a constant glow. Then he had spoken, firmly ordering them to stand in front of the cart in a line. He knew what they were doing, he said, he didn't need to look in the cart.

Then he had begun to stride up and down and to look at them closely. They, as one, had gazed at the revolver in his hand and the dull reflections of the lamplight on the dull metal. He had paced back and forth nearly a hundred times it seemed and he had not said any more.

They had stood frightened, not knowing what was to happen to them. Perhaps even Major Desailles had not known. At any rate, when he had seen Major Villier, some time after she and the others had, he had gestured for him to come closer. For a second Major Villier had just stood there on the edge of the lamplight, and looked at them, especially Celine. Then his head turned and his muscles moved inside his heavy coat.

"What is it sir?"

"Don't be a fool. They're taking *bodies* from the graves. You *told* them about the refused warrants, I suppose."

She could see Major Desailles' jaw tighten and his skin shift to contain it as he looked down the line again. Major Villier looked over their shoulders at what was visible of the cart. The tarpaulin was fastened down over the coffins. Even the smell of the bodies was fading. It was as though, she tried to make him think, they had already gone. If that was so, he had to end Major Desailles' interference.

She could feel that the others were startled by the intensity with which she focused on the pale skin of his face, but she had to let him know. She had known the feeling in him when he had resolved to help them. She filled up with the desperate urge to succeed and end the chain of defeats that had overwhelmed her and the village and tried to make him feel it. How could he not? His very actions had proved the level of understanding of which he was capable. But still he stood and stared, and deferred to the authority of the man with the gun in his hand.

"Are you are sure, sir?"

"Yes, *damn* it! I've been *waiting* for you to arrive so you can assist in the arrest. Draw your revolver and stop standing there like an *idiot!*"

At the word "revolver" he looked down at his empty hand as though he was surprised. Then he looked slowly up again and gazed directly at Celine. Perhaps it was the opposing pressures, she thought. She wanted him to act; Major Desailles wanted him to act, and he had taken refuge in inactivity. But he must act! This thought shot through all of them. Its energy caused them almost to step towards the two officers.

Major Desailles started at the movement and his gun jerked towards them again, then his eyes, and he frowned as though contemplating a summary execution. And this movement, the nervousness of the group and the angry response of the solitary man, made Major Villier decide.

He took one last look at Celine and pulled his revolver out of its holster. Celine could feel every person in that circle of light holding their breath to see where he would point it. All the eyes focussed on the little lump of metal as it slowly emerged from the leather holster, and straightened in his hand, and pointed… it pointed straight at Celine.

For a second they all gazed at the barrel and the lines of orange that reflected from it. Each of them instinctively put out a hand as though to protect themselves. Celine stood open-mouthed, then turned her face to his to find out what he had thought to bring this change about in him, what had so hidden her from him so that he would obey Major Desailles.

But in his face there was no hint of obedience to Major Desailles. The gun was directed at them but his eyes took in only Major Desailles.

"What happens if they run sir?"

His voice was not dull as it had been, but sharp and clear. Still the group trembled, but now Major Desailles looked away from them to him, in surprise at his new tone.

"*Why* did I ask you to draw your revolver?"

"To shoot them if they try to run?"

"Very good. Now *listen*…"

"What if she runs sir?"

In a few quick steps he had seized Celine by the shoulder, pushing through the group to grasp her roughly. She tried to move her shoulder out from his tight grip, never having expected such cruelty in his fingers. She felt the metal of the gun on her temple, cold and unpleasant, but it was the fingers that made her most afraid.

"Shall I shoot her then sir?"

"Don't be such an *idiot*. Let her *go*, you fool."

"Very well, sir."

The tight fingers were gone, but she could still sense his body just behind her; his clothes brushed against her back. She knew then. She understood what he had done. He had not barged into the group – he had joined them, and joined her, taken hold of her as his support.

Major Desailles was left on the other side of the circle of light, away from the coffins, and the revolver was slipping out of his fingers, falling, making only a soft sound against the mud.

Over her shoulder she could feel Major Villier's arm outstretched, and at the end of it the gun, trembling a little – the light moved to and fro on its surface – but now pointing at Major Desailles. He had dropped his revolver, now he let his arm fall to his side. His face was contorted with fear and anger; his throat moved but only a faint hissing of released breath came from his throat.

Now Major Villier looked left and right at faces that were still pale, but which, Celine knew, covered feelings of the most intense relief. She saw him smile a long slow smile as though he had finally found something he had dreamed about. Then his face grew serious again and he looked back at Major Desailles.

"Come here, Major. I won't shoot you – unless you run away."

Major Desailles carried on looking at the gun. Then, as though he were some kind of magician he turned his blue-coated back to them and he was gone out of the circle of light. Major Villier took two or three long strides after him, his boots sounding loud on the earth and his arm still held out rigidly before him, the gun barrel now pointing at nothing. He stopped and dropped his arm. He looked around him in a bewildered manner before seeing Celine. As he did so they could hear the scampering steps of Major Desailles suddenly come to an abrupt stop as though their cause had fallen into one of the newly opened graves.

Now that Major Villier had seen Celine he seemed to come to himself. Still looking at her he shrugged as if to say "I'm sorry". But she had no need of his apologies. She glowed with pride in him for what he had done for her, and for Jean-Paul.

After his shrug he went forward the rest of the distance to where Major Desailles had stood and picked up his revolver. For a second he looked idly at the two guns in his hand while she and the others watched, impatient to be moving, to have left Pericard, but afraid to begin to act without him. But then the need to hurry communicated itself to him. He turned and spoke quietly, not wasting his breath.

"I think that you men, except for anyone who is to drive the cart, should go back to the village. I don't think, when they start hunting me, that they'll bother too much with you. Everyone else – I hope you have everything with you because you should go – now."

The men who were not coming with them bid a hasty farewell and ran off into the darkness carrying their digging tools with them. Celine looked at them as they went, hoping that they would not encounter any pursuers, but it seemed that Major Villier had already stopped thinking about them.

He hurried forward and took up the lamp, which swung unsteadily from his hand. He went with it round to the horses and with his other hand felt the traces and harness to make sure that they were secure. Meanwhile the others climbed aboard – the two drivers, the six women. None of them had yet spoken, but as Celine watched she saw each of them cross themselves and offer up a short prayer when they stepped near the tarpaulin-shrouded coffins.

As they sat, Major Villier lifted up the lamp so that the light he held could be taken up into the cart. As he did so there was suddenly an outbreak of speech, blessings, thanks, exclamations that blurred over each other and became a babble. He brushed them aside with a hand and looked again at the passengers.

It was then she realised with a start that he was looking for her, as though he had not expected her to wait down here to thank him individually. She stepped forward quickly and touched his arm with a trembling hand. His face was pale as he looked round. She smiled at him and offered to embrace him but he leaned forward and whispered ashamedly in her ear.

"I couldn't put him, Desailles I mean, in your husband's place."

He stared at her, seeming to want some response to this ambiguity – was he being respectful or merciful? She frowned but then nodded.

"I understand."

He seemed relieved. But her heart was beating faster because she felt the fear of those in the carriage. She would never risk her husband's body again, not even for his man to whom she owed so much in gratitude. She smiled at him and glanced up at the cart. He saw the glance, as he was supposed to, but it seemed he did not act on it. Instead he drew her into his arms and placed a single kiss on her forehead. Then, in a sudden access of strength she felt him strain his arms with his hands on her waist, and lift her onto the cart, seating her on the edge of the coffin-covering tarpaulin. She felt the gratitude of them all swell up inside her as she rejoined them but he had let his eyes drop from her as though he was afraid of being caught looking now that she was with her husband again. Though his eyes were directed to the ground he was able to raise his voice.

"Ride on!"

The driver slapped the reins without hesitation and the cart lurched forward leaving the major outside the pool of light cast by the lamp. He seemed to be incredibly distant almost immediately, remaining for a short time a grey figure only just visible standing still, appearing to watch them. Then, as the horses picked up speed, he was gone.

Celine carried on watching for a moment after he disappeared in case she could tell what had happened to him, but then, despite a lingering wish to catch one last glimpse of him, she turned her head. None of the women in the cart would be looking out for him for long, not because they wanted to forget, but because now they carried with them bodies that were more vital even than memories.

Marie began to pray again, hurriedly, fervently, eager to express all her thanksgiving, present and yet to come, before she reached Paris. There was a strange, sad joy in them all which was made all the more confused by having to leave Pericard and everything there.

Celine began to slip her hands under the tarpaulin. She knew which coffin was Jean-Paul's by its feel, and the feeling that she had when she was near it, the feeling that she was close to him as he had been. In Pericard, she knew, he still waited. In Pericard he had died, and so she was almost afraid to leave it because it had so much of Jean-Paul and, for a short time at least, it still contained him as he was now, one form of him that was real.

But the strange longing she could not suppress for the mud and the low huts of the village was greatly outweighed by this new reality of Jean-Paul – his body, having possession of him again. He had told the truth. She believed him now.

"I will come back. Look what I have to come back to."

She had her hands on the coffin, feeling the earth that still adhered to it and he himself, inside, alive, living as he had done before the war and in her mind during it. Look! He was there now, smiling, reaching out his hands to her. She had done what she promised. Soon her husband would be home. His memory would be given what it most desired from life, and he would always be with her.

Yet as she thought these things she knew that Major Villier would still be in her thoughts. The impression of his kiss was still on her physical forehead and she remembered his frightened eyes as he had tried to explain why he had not killed Major Desailles. As she dreamed of and felt the presence of Jean-Paul, she was aware of him lingering on the edge of her thoughts just as he had lingered on the edge of the light as the cart pulled away from him. She knew now that he understood, that, almost too late, he had learned to understand the acceptance and the pain of loss that she herself knew too well. She shuddered. His was another soul ruined by the war. When she buried her husband's body in the churchyard at home she would light a candle for Major Villier.

Ricard

"*Where* have they gone?"

"Rheims."

The slap turned his head to the side. He turned it back, believing that it should have stung, that he should have felt the wind of it. Instead he looked steadily at Desailles without flinching. The major was speaking again. Ricard could see and hear the anger on his face and in his voice, but on the whole it made little impression on him. Physical things and their impressions were all distant, as the slap had been, as if he had been in some strange way able to see it administered to someone else.

"I *know* they're going to Rheims. Where *else* would they go?"

"I don't know."

"*Damn* it! You *do*! The whole scheme was *yours*."

"I helped them go. I'm not their keeper."

Desailles paused again and Ricard paused with him. He had begun to see his new sensations as a blessing. Wrapped up in their cocoon, he was certain in his belief that Celine would manage to get away. He would lose her, it was true, but even here, even in the Pericard of Desailles' dominion, he was helping her by leading him astray. And the new sensations gave him the strength he needed, he knew.

Desailles was speaking again, to the sergeant he had brought with him. Ricard ignored the sounds and ran his mind over the shift in his experience. It had been terrifying at first, beginning slowly as the cart had lurched away from him. He had felt lost, as, really, he had expected, but then as lost within himself, almost searching for Celine inside his own mind.

Then he had run, run at the village, and saw the lights of pursuers coming from it. To his overwrought mind they were almost like comets or the shells he had seen fired as signals from ships near Grenon. He had encountered them, the pursuers, with a sense that he was still on Grenon, running an exercise for his men, firing over their heads, running and hiding as they scattered, and then the same again and again, not feeling that they might kill him. It was only after they had caught him, running him to ground in a wide circle that the reality of death's danger had occurred – and it occurred to him in a way that didn't matter. It was as if he had floated, as they bound his hands, on a cloud of fear at that time. He feared that he was mad, that Celine's departure had divorced him from his senses. He had understood what was happening only later, when he had recalled what she had tried to explain to him and remembered her dedication to her husband that did not require her own comfort. What she had done was for him. What he, Ricard, was doing was for her. It made sense at last.

Desailles was staring at him again but Ricard's thoughts wandered away to the memorials on the newly stained battlefield. He remembered Jannert's words to him – what arose from today he would deal with. He suspected that out there tonight there would be more memorials. All those rifles and helmets added to the sombre line in the trench. As it should be, as it should be... each man his own mark. And the other memorials – there would be more silver things, little jewels on the gun emplacement, perhaps even where the men died at Vellard's stronghold.

Ricard became lost in these images and gradually realised that he did not suspect them to be true – he knew. He knew as certainly as if his hands had performed the

222

actions themselves rather than Jannert's. It was as though if he had looked away from the slap Desailles gave him he would have seen, from the same vantage point, Jannert forming the new markers for the dead men.

"…but I suppose at any rate I have *you* here. I can make an *example* of you too. You *won't* have to wait too long. *Sergeant*, take him to the infirmary. Put him in with the other two."

"Yes sir."

Ricard's mind was far more jolted by this tail end of his interview with Desailles than his body was by the firm pressure of the sergeant's hand. But he had little time to think of what he was to fear from Vellard and Noilly since he was quickly led across the main central space of the village. Villagers and soldiers stopped to look at him but he did not read their faces, only their feelings – fear and pity. Fear of what might befall them if he, their commander, could be so imprisoned, and pity because as he was clearly aware they all knew of, and sympathised with, what he had tried to do – had done – for Celine and those others.

He recognised some of the men and they turned towards him with secretive smiles on their lips. But they could do nothing. It was not averted then, the closing of the guarded door that sealed him in with Vellard and Noilly. Nor was the room altered for him either by the guards or the inmates. In all respects it was dark. Ricard tried to find somewhere to sit in the gloom, but crashed against a little table and something else before his fingers touched the cold metal corrugations of the wall. The bruises he might have received, and the noise he was aware of making were however secondary in his thoughts. He was afraid that those very thoughts would awaken Vellard's which would take some unguessed revenge on him.

But the danger did not appear. The new blessings did

not turn against him, for Vellard's mind remained as unilluminated to him as it always had been. The catatonia he had observed before in the body seemed to have taken hold of the mind. Ricard could feel the many impulses from the village more plainly than anything from Vellard and Noilly. He moved along the wall with his fingers, guessing from impressions that seemed second-hand where the window was, where the edge of the blanket that covered it. He let in some light.

They lay as they had done before, almost like effigies that had remained there for centuries so that the inquisitive could come and peer at their faces. The eyes beneath the lids did not move as the light fell on them, but, as though it lit up their thoughts with its feeble glow, Ricard sensed something vague and shadowy in them that lost its form as he tried to focus on it. Slowly he sat down and looked out of the window to where the minds of Pericard moved and for a while he sat between the two motionless forms and barely sensed anything at all.

When, eventually, he brought his mind to order again the glimmer of something from Vellard had faded. He stood, went over and looked down at the unmoving face with its thin, seemingly transparent, skin. He was surprised that even in sleep Lieutenant Vellard should be so lacking in the feelings that he himself, and apparently everyone else in Pericard, was so aware of. If anyone should have access to such a level of awareness, it should be Vellard. He thought hard about the emotive fires in the young man. Surely here was a man who understood clearly what it would be to act for those who could no longer act. And Noilly too…?

Even as he thought these things he knew that the answer was obvious. Vellard and his companion were dead. Though they still breathed – just – their bodies and minds considered themselves dead along with all the others who had died. Vellard's three wounds had helped persuade him of his own death. Like the very shallowness of his breathing, the formless flicker that Ricard seized on in his mind was simply that of a machine ticking over. Ricard recoiled from it as he had recoiled from the body he had encountered on his first visit to the battlefield. Something alien and dead... rotted, decayed. Ricard put space between himself and the recumbent man. He stood at the window again and tried to lose himself in the village. Here the image of Celine was recalled to him and the trembling that provoked in his eyes and mind enabled him to forget the two inaccessible things that still lay in the half-light behind him.

Captain Deschaves interrupted him. Captain Deschaves, bandaged, drained, looking ten years older. He pushed the door open with his good arm so that it banged loudly against the wall. Ricard turned in surprise. The sleepers did not move. Deschaves looked at each of them with a strange kind of smile on his lips. Then he turned to Ricard.

"Bit of an insult, don't you think?"

"What?"

"You – and him in the same room. Both under arrest."

"I suppose it is."

Deschaves' lips were almost white and he licked them again and again. Then he reached under the long folds of his greatcoat with his healthy hand and pulled out a book. He weighed it carefully in his hand and then extended his arm to Ricard.

"*Les Miserables*. Lieutenant Jannert suggested I give it to you before he left. He said it whiled away the hours."

Ricard did not take it. Suddenly he missed Jannert and his patience. Deschaves looked at him for a while and then let the book fall to the floor.

"You finally believed her then?"

"Who? Madame Delain? Wasn't she right after all?"

"Hm."

Deschaves pulled a peculiar face and began to wander back and forth.

"I know what you thought of her. Suddenly you can understand, whereas I – You don't know what made him shoot at me do you?"

He stepped over Vellard's couch again and looked down. Ricard watched him, getting an inkling of what Deschaves was talking about. He sensed nothing from him other than what he could see, hear and smell. Something lost... Why had Deschaves come to see him?

"Whereas you...?"

"It doesn't matter. I'm here out of interest, you know. I'm interested in how you two – you and him – rub along together. All right, I see. Do you know what he knows? Has he told you? Did you tell him you understood, and he told you the answer? Tell me, perhaps. What happens at the end of the trenches?"

"Captain Deschaves – I think you're fevered. You can't have got over your wound yet – Captain Deschaves! Calm yourself. Please! You..."

Ricard offered no resistance. Deschaves had pushed him up to the wall and rested on him with the lower point of his front arm. The face of the captain was close to his own and the pressure of the arm was against his chest and almost, through the dislocation between his mind and his body, hurting him. Ricard felt no fear, only curiosity now as the captain's face ran with sweat and he demanded what he wanted to know again in a voice controlled only with the greatest effort.

"Did – he tell you – what happened when – the trenches ended? Did he decide to you trust you with that?"

Ricard looked into his eyes for a long time, trying to

work out what he was thinking, if anything. When he spoke, he found, oddly, that his voice was constricted. Perhaps Deschaves was strangling him.

"No. How could he? He hasn't moved. And anyway, what does it matter? I don't know, so why should you?"

Deschaves let him go. He didn't even look at him, just simply let his arm and his eyes drop. With his other arm in the sling he looked vulnerable and weak. Ricard put out a hand to tap him, to make him look up, or react in some way. But before the outstretched fingers, which Ricard watched with detached interest, could straighten enough to finish their journey, Deschaves had already reacted. He stalked back across to the other side of the room and stared down at Vellard again. Then he spat onto his face. The saliva did not shoot out of his mouth with any venom. It simply dribbled in a long string. When he had finished he turned to Ricard. His face barely seemed to move as he spoke.

"In time you will realise how right you were, and I am now. France can't go on living inside his head."

Ricard thought he saw the face begin to fold into tears. But Deschaves had turned away. The wound in his shoulder restricted his movements and so he shambled. Ricard watched him without understanding, but after the door had closed he followed in those slow footsteps as far as Vellard's bedside. As he wiped Deschaves' spit from the face of the young lieutenant he was aware of copying again, not Deschaves this time, but Celine. As he cleaned the face of the unconscious man he was imitating the moves she would have made to clean the face of the wounded men lying in other parts of the infirmary. He *knew* she would act like this for those who could comprehend her fate. He acted this way for her because she would understand him.

Next morning he awoke with a start. Lieutenant Georges was already in the room squeezing water from sponges between the lips of the two men. Ricard leapt up from the chair in which he had sat for some sixteen hours, not feeling the aches, but only aware of the emotional noise from the village and within himself. As he had grown used to his sensations he had begun to train his feelings more, sensing what was in the minds of this or that group. Always at the root of it, some sense of something missing, not retrievable, something like the loss of Celine.

He had not bent his mind to the soldiers who were closest to him, on just the other side of the wall. He guessed that if he had concentrated his ears he would have heard enough. He was afraid of what he would find if he turned to them, with their wounds and injured limbs. There was loss too immediate even for him to bear. If he was given time – well, perhaps. For the moment he was simply aware of Lieutenant Georges' patience as he tended to the bodily needs of the two dead men.

"Can I help you?"

"No, sir. It's all right. They don't take much looking after."

"What's wrong with them?"

"Your guess is as good as mine, sir. I'm sorry sir, I must go. But I shall ask Major Desailles to send you some food. You need it too, you know."

The patience, the kindness and bloodstained hands. Ricard closed his eyes and tried to draw his mind into itself, so that it should not have to face the whole reality. Lieutenant Georges was a braver man than he. There was none of the resentment in him that had finally spurred Ricard to act for Celine. The desire in him to act for the lost ones was a calm, kind one. Ricard was irritated with himself. Lieutenant Georges, however admirable, was still Lieutenant Georges. He was Ricard. He acted for Celine.

When the doctor had gone Ricard sensed something else, almost like the aftertaste left by pungent wine, or the battlefields now after the war. There was another sadness in there that Ricard had not noticed. But once he noticed it there he noticed it everywhere. In the village, something else was being lost. He could not begin to work out what it was. For a few minutes he worried at the feeling, almost shaking it about in his head in case something dropped out of it – an image, an idea. Then, defeated, he bent and picked up the book that Deschaves had let fall. He flipped quickly through the pages.

Then – at his back! Something was there, something awesome. The book fell again and Ricard turned, knowing that when his face had presented itself to Vellard again things would have changed. Vellard's eyes were open. And where Ricard had only sensed something little before, a churning of feelings, a tempest of sensations poured over his body.

He reeled from it, unable to separate any one impression from another. His senses still worked – on the other side of the room Noilly too was gazing from open eyes. The eyes though did not move, as if the owners were still in their long trance. Ricard's eyes, moving between them, watched with animal instincts. His mind was still crushed by the whirling collection of feelings bursting out without form from the prostrate bodies. Without his noticing it his body began to droop, lowering him down to the cold wooden floor of the room.

There it was clearer, as the air, he remembered, was supposed to be clearer beneath the clouds of gas as they drifted over the trenches. There he could attempt to view what he felt from a little distance. Yet as he tried to grasp it, it seized him again and he felt drawn into the cloud, almost oblivious, but cursed through a little knowledge – he knew the cloud had pain in it, and fear, and disgust. The feelings, now that he was aware of them, ate into him there, ate into him, and he almost put out his hands to protect himself as a man fired at feebly tries to shield his flesh from the bullet. He thought he screamed.

He knew this place well. The contours of the ground, the arrangement here and there of barbed wire, shell holes – but it was unfamiliar. He concentrated and smelt the air, and knew why. Though it was as silent as he had always known it, the battlefield looked *newer*. The old scars he remembered were here open wounds, the areas his men had trawled, shuffling in long lines to collect the rubbish and so make the tiniest of impressions on the earth were, if anything, even more littered with debris. He stood up and the smell redoubled, not the combined stink he knew so well, but separate ones – shit, rotting flesh, piss, rotting clothes, the mud itself. He could have taken the air apart and pinpointed the source of each stench. The smell he knew well could never be so dismantled. Decay created new combinations as it destroyed the old.

He turned towards where he knew there would be trenches and his suspicions were confirmed. The parapets, which he only knew as collapsing heaps of sandbags, were built up, firm and black instead of the dull dripping grey the clouds had made them in Pericard. This was the battlefield as it had been, long before he came to it, where the entombed men still fought.

Carefully, feeling his feet slip in mud that had not yet congealed, he moved closer.

After only a few steps a sound caught his ear. A human sound. His hand went to his revolver. He had forgotten that he had been disarmed. He went towards the sound nonetheless.

"Vellard! Private Noilly!"

They looked up once but then their eyes were trained on the earth again. They knelt in a shell hole, hands raised in prayer, heads bowed in submission. Their clothes hung about them like the rags on one of the corpses inadvertently buried out here. They faced the trenches, perhaps begging whatever mysterious deity that watched over them for some favour. Ricard watched, then moved closer. He watched again. Their faces did not move, and as he looked more carefully he revised his opinion. They were not praying – they were waiting. And then, maybe, when they had waited, they would pray.

He turned back to the trenches. There was an air of expectancy about them, too, though as soon as he thought this he tried to scrabble thought out of his mind. This was sheer fantasy. He moved forward, but afraid now, terrified by his fantastic imagination.

A whistle, in the distance. Another, another, another, shooting along the line of the trench closest to him, the front line trench. Within seconds the sounds had shot past him and on, on into the edges of the battlefield. Then the helmets, climbing to the top of the ladders, on his left. An assault. The war!

He ran, stumbling from the rows of helmets that bobbed slowly upwards on ladders that followed the line of the whistle. He reached Vellard, fell into the man, knocking him off his knees sideways and back, away from the trenches. With one push Vellard dislodged him. The lieutenant lurched back and got back into his posture of supplication. Ricard watched.

The soldiers were almost upon them now, bayonets fixed, but not firing. The whole event, after the whistles, took place in total, ear-straining silence except for the sounds of boots in mud. Not a gun fired, no officer shouted, no men screamed and fell writhing to the earth. Yet it was an attack – there was no sense of this being a training exercise.

Ricard saw their faces and his understanding fell

completely into place. These were the dead of Pericard. Eyeless, skinless faces, some with strips of green gangrenous flesh hanging down over exposed tooth-stumps. Ricard could feel the agony of the individuals and the collective pain – he covered his eyes while they all ran past him. These were the dead, and he could hear and feel their feet thudding into the earth in the midst of this long-silent battlefield.

Then one stopped. Ricard cowered for a little longer but at last, without really knowing why, he took his hands away from his eyes and looked up. It was an officer, he guessed, from the revolver. There was a gaping wound in the chest surrounded by blood-stiff cloth. Rats had gnawed at its face, taking an eye. The one that remained, bright and somehow still alive, regarded him slowly. Ricard dared not move, even though the revolver barrel had dipped towards the earth. It was a long gaze this dead officer gave him. After a while Ricard could smell his trench-breath, but he did not flinch. Locked in this gaze, he felt that something was being communicated to him, though what it was he did not know. But at last the dead officer looked away, or turned, and he was gone, running in the wake of his comrades. Ricard levered himself into a sitting position and shifted his legs so that they no longer hurt him and watched him go.

A quiet groan cut into his infant reflections on the gaze he had been favoured with, or subjected to. He turned at once and saw Vellard crawling, tears and snot pouring from his face. Nearby Noilly simply sat, ashen-faced. Crawling himself, Ricard pushed forward. He tried to take hold of Vellard's coat but the lieutenant shook him off. Defeated, he looked about him. The dead men had gone. Already the sharp edges of the battlefield were decaying, becoming the cloying mud he knew so well.

A sense of the desolation of it that he had never felt

before washed over him. It was not merely that civilisation had been destroyed by it, it was that now the dead men had gone, had abandoned all that was left for them to possess, civilisation could never exist here again. Ricard shot a despairing look at the sandbags as if hoping that some assistance might still come from there, and crawled back to Vellard. But the lieutenant was vomiting, bile and blood, curled up on himself like barbed wire not yet laid out. Ricard shook him and slapped him but the young man took no notice, wrapped up as he was in the wave of grief.

Later, sitting in the silent room in the still village, he felt the roughness of the pillow still tingling through his fingers. He had been in the room again and felt the last of his new sensations draining, with the others in the village, like a tide towards the battlefield. He put up no resistance. He was sure that no-one else in the village had resisted either. How could you resist? Run screaming after them crying "Give me you back"? Resist angrily like Captain Deschaves? Ricard had his senses again and he had looked out on Pericard with surprised eyes.

The first spring of peace since 1914 had warned of its arrival in a brief burst of sunshine. The clouds had since returned but by their light Ricard had read parts of *Les Miserables* for the first time while the flesh of his fingers, grazed by the coarse material of the pillowcase, had gradually stopped stinging so much.

His first action on finding himself in the prison-room again had been to pluck the pillow from under the head of Vellard and press it to his face. Vellard had not reacted while Ricard smothered him. Nor had Private Noilly when his turn came. When both bodies were dead he replaced the pillow under the lieutenant's head.

Now that was done and Ricard was entirely alone. Even Jannert would have taken his train to Verdun by now.

So *Les Miserables* was all he had while he sat between the two corpses and waited for Desailles' threats to become action. But when they did they would be toothless dangers, for by then Lieutenant Vellard and Private Noilly would have been taken from this room and buried in Pericard's military cemetery alongside those they had tried to follow.

Ricard picked up his book and read on, but with no great concentration. In his mind's eye Celine and her husband made stately progress towards their home.

Celine – 1939

She had known it was him the day before as she had hurried home from the village school against the driving rain. He had been staring at the war memorial in the central square and reading the names of the fallen. She had not seen his face, but there was something in the way he carried himself... and besides, no-one ever looked at the memorial any more, except in November.

The next morning, Saturday, she woke earlier than usual and dressed, putting on tight shoes which clacked on the cobbles of the street and sent little echoes ricocheting from wall to wall disturbing the families still asleep. There was a heavy mist lingering between the houses as though planning an ambush on the winter light tentatively flickering in the sky. He was still at the memorial, sleeping apparently without discomfort beneath the scroll of carved names. With her eyes she ran down the list, reading information she already knew well: "Delain, Lieutenant Jean-Paul; 153rd".

She reached down and lightly touched the sleeping man on his unshaven cheek. His flesh was hard as though he had spent the time since they had last been together facing into a cold wind.

"Major Villier?"

He opened his eyes with a surprised grunt and wiped saliva from his thick lips. He no longer had a moustache and under the loose cap on his head his hair had thinned. As he focused on her he broke into a nervous smile. He began to speak but found himself stuttering slowly rather than forming words. She crouched beside him and pulled the two sides of the blanket he wore tight around him so that his heavy hands, covered with scars, were concealed.

"H-hello C- Celine?"

She helped him get to his feet, feeling the extra weight of his bulk after all the years. His lips were stained in one place from where he held his rolled-up cigarettes, and his face was made up of jigsaw pieces separated by thin breaks. He was cold. She wanted to take him inside before the rain fell again, but first he insisted on turning back to the names and underlining Jean-Paul's with his finger. She looked away from his eyes but nodded. Then she led him back through the mist-coated streets to her little flat above Jean-Paul's cousin's bakery.

Once inside he seemed to come alive again and ran his finger along the spines of the schoolbooks she had arranged in a corner. She made coffee. He asked no questions but took off his coat and hung it next to the stove to ease some of the dampness from its folds. They were silent until they had sat down opposite each other with their coffee. Then he began to speak, not, as she had expected, like a man learning to talk again after long years of silence, but easily and with animation.

"I came to bring you a book."

"Really?"

"Yes. This one."

He reached under the edge of the blanket that was still wrapped around him and produced a bag into which he dug with one hand until he extracted, in triumph, a large book.

"People think it's a Bible, but it's not, it used to belong to Captain Deschaves. He found it in a German trench. He gave it to me the day after you left Pericard. *Les Miserables*."

"It's been a bit of an effort to bring me a book hasn't it?"

She leafed through the pages. One or two dropped out and fell limply into her lap. She smiled and put them back into the volume. She put one hand to her greying hair and then stopped, struck by a half-mischievous impulse. She got up and took the book across the room, over to the fireplace. There she picked up a photograph frame and put the book beneath it, its spine facing outwards into the room. Then she turned to face Major Villier. She saw him make an effort to bring the photograph into focus. At length he got up and shuffled his way over the floorboards and close to her. She moved the photograph so that he could see it more easily. When he realised who it was he laughed, or at least snorted, and began to shuffle back to his coffee.

"So that's what he looked like in life. You know, I never realised I didn't know."

She looked at him in concern as she straightened Jean-Paul's photograph. His voice had not regained its old strength despite the energy he put into it. Seeing him now she could hardly believe she had recognised him, he was so stooped.

"Why have you taken so long to deliver a book?"

"In the asylum…"

He seemed not to want to continue but her silence made him carry on.

"I told them what I'd seen – I won't need to describe it to you… I'm sure you would be able to understand – and Desailles and Deschaves got me… locked up. Captain Deschaves had already told me that I couldn't pretend France was in Lieutenant Vellard's head any more."

"I suppose they were right."

"Yes, yes they were right. I was right when I came to Pericard – clear it up, let people get on with their lives again. Which is all very civilised, but…"

She smiled and did not answer him. He sighed and drained his coffee cup. He looked at her with a crooked grin playing about his lips.

"It doesn't matter. I think in the end it was inevitable."

"Inevitable? Maybe. How did you find me?"

"Perseverance. I knew to try near Bordeaux and so…"

He looked at her shyly as he spoke. She looked away from his gaze again and began to wonder if, in the long stretches of the night just past between seeing him and coming to meet him, she had made a mistake. She stood. Her faith in him was not broken, but she wanted to test him. Her own mind would be set at rest as well. She had not stopped thinking about him. He followed her with his eyes but he seemed to guess what was in her mind and stood up too.

"Take me to him then."

He pulled the blanket tighter around him and forced the coat on over it. He followed her down her narrow wooden back staircase and out on to the street again. It was still early but one or two people were moving about the streets. Somewhere nearby a car engine was bullied into life. Its turning provided an undertone to their own private thoughts as they made their way without speaking to the church. Its tall windows and heavy wooden doors were still sealed at this time in the morning, but Celine swung the little gate to the churchyard back without difficulty. She let him through first. He moved slowly, his age and incarceration combining to keep his movements controlled, restrained. She watched the side of his face, saw the muscles move under the leathery skin as his eyes moved back and forth amongst the jumble of tombstones. She saw them stop at each bundle of flowers, then move on, back and forth. Hesitantly she reached out and touched his arm. He left off looking with reluctance.

She felt every line in her face as she smiled tightly at him and saw his face concentrate all its attention on her.

"This way."

Through the tombstones she went, still lightly resting

her fingers on his elbow. She led him on and on towards the back of the space, where weeds from outside the village seemed ready to sweep forward and engulf the whole place. Then he saw the bunch of flowers and she felt his body stiffen. He crossed himself. After twenty years – almost exactly – she still knew him.

She brought him closer so that his fading eyes could make out the markings on the stone: "Beloved husband Jean-Paul DELAIN Bordeaux 1891-Pericard 1917 Buried here March 1919". Major Villier crossed himself and bowed his head briefly. She saw his eyes wander from the letters to the clipped bramble ends that framed the tombstone. He went forward and touched one with his big fingers. She knew he was acknowledging what she had done even after her husband had been set at rest. She had, for twenty years, kept him still with her, and kept the war with her.

He stood beside her again, looking at her with old eyes. She stammered as she spoke.

"Otherwise they – everyone – forget. The memorial – it's just names now."

He nodded, and seemed to laugh at the irony. Then he looked back at the grave.

"I saw him."

"When?"

"When they left. He ran past me and stopped. I think he was thanking me. I didn't thank him."

She shrugged. She paused, looking at her husband's grave. Then at him, expectantly. This was the moment of the test. He seemed unaware of it, simply stared back across the few feet of space. He straightened his back suddenly, military style.

"Thank you."

He saluted in the slow deliberate way she had come to expect. Without the twitch of a muscle in his face he bid her farewell and came no closer to her. She let out a long pent-up breath and felt her shoulders slacken. He still understood. He had passed. But the passing was almost as painful as the failing would have been. His shadowy presence would go for ever. She would be the old war-widow again, alone and gradually forgotten.

She stepped back and to the side a little as if letting him past. With straight shoulders and still eyes he began to move past her, back into the main body of the churchyard. As he did so he could not help looking at her one last time. With hardly a thought she put out both her hands and laid them gently on each cheek just below his eyes. She strained her body, feeling muscles stretch in her legs and back as she stood on tiptoe. He realised what she was doing and lowered his forehead to within her reach. She pressed her lips to the old, wrinkled skin. Her husband was a witness again, as he had been to the first part of the exchange. She held him like that for a few seconds, then released him and came back down to her normal height. She saw that the kiss had done to him what a simple parting had not been able. She wiped away the silvery tear-trails with her fingers, then brought her hand up to her own eye.

"So – where'll you go now?"

He shrugged, showing yellowing teeth in a smile that was mixture of grief and something like a celebration of liberation.

"Don't know. Perhaps... Pericard? Should be quite a pretty little village by now."

"Yes."

It was a choking kind of laugh. He looked at her strangely for a second, then turned his back to her, and was gone. She could see his figure – yes it did still retain some of the old way that he moved – passing between the masses of gravestones, the outline of his form growing less and less distinct as the mist flowed in like a silent sea between them. She saw him reach the gate, heard the metal of it clink into place as it closed. Then she could see him no longer even though she was certain of him moving slowly through the waking streets of the village. A known shape in a known place, but inaccessible. She turned back to the known shape of her husband's tombstone.

Kneeling at the foot of it, ignoring the coldness of the earth, she rearranged the red flowers in their little pot. Tears fell on to the shrivelled and crumpled petals as she did so. When the frosts returned each petal and tear would drop and shatter on the hard ground. When she had finished, she stood and felt the brush of her husband's hand down her back. In the church the candles she had lit for both men had long since melted into heaps of unformed wax. She would go again before mass. She would light another candle for her husband. She would light another candle for Major Villier.

As the rooks and crows gathered in the treetops and on the roofs of the houses in the early light of the morning she walked away from her husband's grave and, alone, made her way back to her tiny rooms in the centre of the village.